Lead your way. Be your own leader!

Lead your way. Be your own leader!

力得文化
Leader Culture

詹宜婷 ◎著

Smart外交英語
從中西諺語的文化交流開始

促進外交，同步提升中英互譯能力的第一步
「中西」溝通零障礙！

Smart學中西諺語的步驟

1. 認識中西諺語的文化背景與趣事，拓展話題廣度不辭窮！
2. 學會中西諺語的用法，穩固中、英文深厚的基底！
3. 吸收與中西諺語相關的其它說法，培養中英互譯、換句話說的思維！
4. 模擬與老外文化交流的3問3答，跟讀MP3同步練習，加強口語流暢度、加快重要場合的反應能力！

循序漸進透過中西文化交流拉近彼此，溝通無國界！

適合**翻譯系所師生**、**有志從事口譯工作者**、

致力於**推廣中文與背後文化的社會人士**

Smart Diplomacy Starts from Chinese and English Idioms

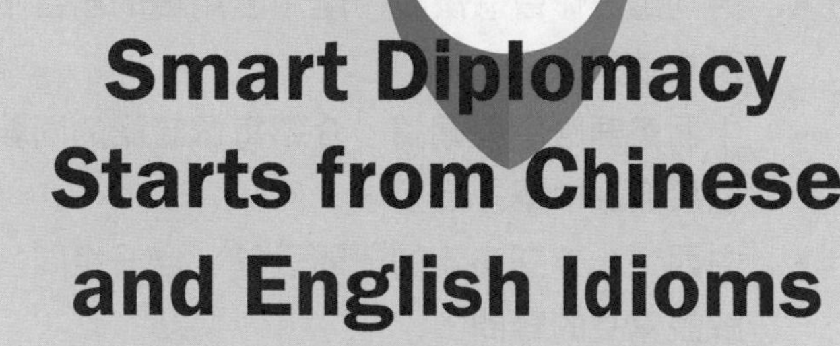

Introduction 作者序

當與國外客戶或朋友對談時，常常會聽到一些不容易由字面來理解的慣用語。其實這些慣用語都有典故，了解其出處及由來後，便能輕鬆記憶。本書精心挑選了三十個耳熟能詳的英語慣用語，以詳盡的解說及豐富的例子，來幫助讀者們融會貫通，並活用於日常會話中。每個單元裡包含了五個主題：

- 這句諺語你會怎麼說、能派上用場的場合：了解每個諺語的解釋，及其運用的場合。
- 中西諺語應用與翻譯：介紹每個諺語的同義字及相似的說法，幫助您於會話中舉一反三。
- 中西文化外交交流的一問三答：含三組問答集，以口語的對話方式解說常見的疑問。
- 重點單字：節錄每個單元的重要單字及片語，並附有容易理解的例子。
- 文化巧巧說：介紹每個諺語的中文用法，及相關的文化趣事。

透過本書，除了能幫助您理解實用的英語慣用語、活用於日常會話中，更可以增加會話的豐富性，讓您的國外客戶及朋友對您刮目相看。

詹宜婷

Words from editor
編者序

中西方文化一直都有共通的地方，這也讓語言學習變得有趣。有時於重要的外交場合上，適時提起中西方的共通之處，不但能引起共鳴，還能推廣中文以及其背後相關文化，可說是一舉數得。

為了能讓有志從事外交交流的讀者能夠全面學習中西方相似的俚俗語，本書於是誕生，並特別規劃一問三答的單元，讀者藉由MP3一同搭配學習，相信必能提升回答問題的反應能力、英文口說能力，更於推廣國民外交上，有大為加分的效果！

編輯部

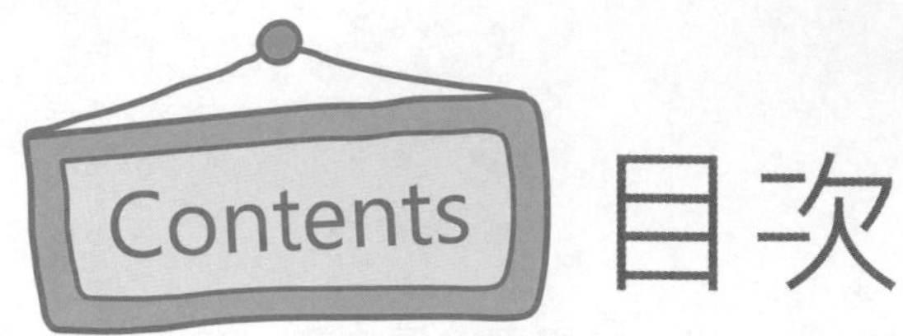

Contents 目次

Chapter Three About Love and Joy
溫馨喜樂篇

Chapter Four About Cultural Communication
中西方文化溝通篇

chapter 1

千古流傳智慧篇

About Wisdom

在英文裡面有「暗箭傷人」的說法嗎？要怎麼和老外介紹我們千古流傳的智慧呢？「暗箭傷人」其實和英文諺語 “Hit below the belt”（意思是在拳賽中攻擊對手腰部以下的地方，衍生為不道德的行為）有異曲同工之妙……原來中西智慧也有這麼相似的地方呢！

Unit 1 A stone's throw (away) 近在咫尺；一箭之遙

How to use this idiom and on what occasions you can use this idiom 這句諺語你會怎麼說、能派上用場的場合

Track 01

A stone's throw (away) means a short distance between two things. Literally speaking it is a distance which can be reached by just throwing a stone. This idiom is very close to the ancient Chinese idioms - 近在咫尺 and 一箭之遙. A stone's throw (away) is commonly used in a variety of situations to indicate a short distance. ***For example, Linda lives just a stone's throw away from her parents. The post office is just a stone's throw away from the city hall.***

A stone's throw (away) 指兩點之間的短程距離。從字面上的意思來看，指非常接近且可用石子投擲就到的距離。這與中文成語- 近在咫尺、一箭之遙的意思不謀而合。***A stone's throw (away) 適合用在表示短距離的各種情況。舉例來說，Linda和父母住的地方僅有一箭之遙。郵局近在咫尺，它就在City hall的附近。***

Synonyms and Analysis 中西諺語應用與翻譯

The original idiom 原來怎麼說

A stone's throw (away)

Synonyms 還能怎麼翻

Nearby, close, within a short distance, around the corner, just a few minutes' walk

Explanations 中西諺語翻譯說明

Another common idiom used to describe distances is around the corner. This idiom is commonly used to describe a short distance between buildings. If something is around the corner, it is very close to where you are and you can easily go to. For example, ***the train station is just around the corner from my office.*** A Chinese idiom-近在咫尺 and around the corner have similar meanings. 咫 and 尺 were used to measure length in ancient China. It denotes a short distance.

Around the corner can also be used to describe something is about to happen shortly. For instance, ***it has thundered several times; heavy rain is just around the corner. With the end of metro construction just around the corner, the house prices near the metro line have gone up sharply.***

另一個形容距離的常用諺語為 Around the corner。這句諺語常用來表示兩棟大樓之間的距離。假如某個事物在 Around the corner，它距離當事人所在的地方非常的近，可輕易到達。舉例來說，***火車站就位在我的辦公室附近***。中文成語的近在咫尺也與 Around the corner 的意思相近。咫、尺在中國古代為用來量測長度，意指短程距離。

Around the corner 也可以用來形容即將要發生的事情。舉例來說，***打了好幾次雷，應該馬上要下大雨了。地鐵工程即將完工，在地鐵線周邊的房價已水漲船高。***

Notes

Analysis 中西諺語翻譯分析

Apart from the idioms above, you can simply describe this situation as *nearby, close, within a short distance, just a few minutes' walk and so on*. You can use nearby as an adjective and an adverb. When you can use *nearby* as an adjective, an example can go like this: ***Stephen walks in a nearby park.*** When you use *nearby* as an adverb, an example can go like this: ***Ben lives nearby.*** *A stone's throw, around the corner, within a short distance* and *just a few minutes' walk* can be put after subjects and verbs in the sentences. For instance, ***the convenient store is just a few minutes' walk.***

除了上述的諺語外，你也可以用簡單的方式來形容，像是 nearby, close, within a short distance, just a few minutes away 等等。當 Nearby 做形容詞時，可這樣運用：***史蒂芬在附近的公園走走***。當 Nearby 做副詞時，可以這麼說：***班住在附近***。A stone's throw, around the corner, within a short distance 及 just a few minutes' walk 等皆可在放在句子中主詞及動詞之後。舉例來說，***便利商店就在路程幾分鐘就能到的地方。***

FAQ 中西文化外交交流的一問三答 Track 02

Q Do you know any similar Chinese idioms describing a short distance?

中文中是否有描述短距離的類似成語？

❶ Well, we often use 近在咫尺 and 一箭之遙. 近在咫尺 is more colloquial but 一箭之遙 is often used in written Chinese.

嗯，我們常用近在咫尺和一箭之遙。近在咫尺為較口語化，而一箭之遙通常用在中文的寫作上。

❷ Yes, we do. People often use 近在咫尺 to talk about a nearby object. 咫 and 尺 were used to measure length in the olden days.

是的，我們有類似的成語。一般人通常用近在咫尺來描述在附近的物品。咫尺在古代為用來量測長度的工具。

❸ You can say 遠在天邊，近在眼前. It describes something is just in front of you but you are not aware of it. It is commonly used in the daily conversation.

你可以說遠在天邊，近在眼前。它是用來形容在你身旁的事物，但你卻不知道。這句很常用在日常生活的對話。

Q What is the difference between *a stone's throw* and *around the corner*?

A stone's throw 和 *Around the corner* 有什麼差別呢？

❶ A stone's throw was an old English idiom derived from the Bible. Around the corner is more colloquial. Both idioms are widely used in daily conversation. In addition, around the corner also means something is coming very soon.

A stone's throw 源自於聖經的一個古老英文諺語。而 Around the corner 較為口語化。兩個諺語皆廣泛的被使用。除此之外，Around the corner 還有指即將來臨的事物。

❷ Well, around the corner is usually used when shops and buildings are not far. A stone's throw can be used in many situations.

嗯，Around the corner通常用來形容商店或大樓在附近，而 A stone's throw 可以運用在各種情況上。

❸ Around the corner means that you can easily go to the other side of a street and find your destination. It is commonly used in daily conversation, such as A: I need to go out to get some groceries. B: The shop is just around the corner.

Around the corner 指就像到對面的街道一樣，你可以輕易地抵達你所要去的目的地。它在日常會話中十分常用。舉例來說，A: 我想要買些食品雜貨。B: 商店就在附近。

Q ***When do you say a stone's throw (from) and when do you say a stone's throw (away)?***
何時用*A stone's throw (from)*，何時用 *A stone's throw (away)* 呢？

❶ If you say something is a stone's throw from, you are talking about a short distance between two places. It goes like A is a stone's throw from B.

假如你使用 A stone's throw from，你是在說明兩個地點之間的短程距離。它可以這樣運用：A is a stone's throw from B.。

❷ You can use either *a stone's throw away from...* or *a stone's throw from....* You can use away or omit it. However, you have to put a specific place, person or thing after "from".

你可用 A stone's throw away from 或者是 A stone's throw from。Away 可保留或省略。但是 from 的後方要接指示的 地點或人物。

❸ Well, when you say *a stone's throw from*, it is usually followed by the place you want to mention. If you don't refer to a distance between two places, you can just say it's only a stone's throw away to indicate it's not far from somewhere.

嗯，當你用 A stone's throw from，它通常會接你想要提及的另一端的地點。假如你沒有要提及兩個地點間的距離，你可以只說 It's only a stone's throw away 來表示距離不遠。

Vocabulary 重點單字

- **denote** *v.* 表示；意思是……

例：Red light in the traffic light denotes an immediate stop.
紅綠燈的紅燈表示立即停止。

- **thunder** *v.* 打雷；雷聲

例：It thundered several times. The noise woke me up.
打雷了好幾聲，聲音吵醒了我。

- **the other side of** *ph.* 另一邊

例：The bus stop is at the other side of the road.
公車站在馬路的另一邊。

- **destination** *n.* 目的地

例：We'll transfer at San Francisco. Our destination is Tokyo.
我們在舊金山轉機，我們的目的地為東京。

- **grocery** *n.* 食品雜貨

例：We usually do our grocery shopping on Saturdays and chill out at home on Sundays.
我們通常週六購買食品雜貨，週日在家放鬆。

- **cultural difference** *n.* 文化差異

例：He has travelled to many countries and is used to the cultural differences.
他到過許多國家旅行，也習慣了文化差異。

- **derive from** *v.* 源自

例：This idiom was derived from an ancient Chinese story.
這句成語源自於一個古老的中國故事。

- **undefined** *adj.* 不明確的

例：This is an undefined task; you need to clarify its job specifications.
這是個不明確的任務，必需清楚說明職務。

文化巧巧說：諺語與外交相關的文化趣事

The relevant phrase of a stone's throw - a stone's cast was originally derived from the Bible and the other relevant phrases had been mentioned in many articles from the sixteenth century.

Both ancient Chinese and English have similar idioms to describe a short distance. A stone's throw is very close to Chinese idioms 一箭之遙 and 近在咫尺. However, they used different objects to measure a short distance due to cultural differences. A stone's throw indicates a short distance which a stone could be thrown, while 一箭之遙 means a distance an arrow could be reached.

Another Chinese idiom- 遠在天邊，近在眼前means something or someone is close to you. However, its meaning is slightly different from 一箭之遙 and 近在咫尺. It denotes that something or someone you have been searching for a long time is actually very close to you. When you talk to your friends or clients, this is an interesting point you could bring up in your conversation.

A stone's throw 的相關詞－a stone's cast 最早出現在聖經裡，其他的相關詞也自十六世紀以來在許多文章中提及。

古代的中國及英國皆有類似的諺語來形容短程的距離。A stone's throw 非常接近中國成語的一箭之遙及近在咫尺。然而，基於文化差異，他們使用不的物體來量測短程距離。A stone's throw 指一顆石子投擲可到達的範圍，而一箭之遙意指一支箭射程的距離。

另一個中文成語－遠在天邊，近在眼前意指非常接近你的某事物。然而，它與一箭之遙及近在咫尺的定義稍為不同。遠在天邊，近在眼前意味著你搜尋已久的某事物，事實上只在你的周圍。當你與朋友或客户對話時，這是你可提起的一個有趣的話題。

Like father, like son
有其父必有其子

How to use this idiom and on what occasions you can use this idiom
這句諺語你會怎麼說、能派上用場的場合

Track 03

This is an ancient proverb describing someone resembles his parents in the way they look or the way they behave. This proverb is often used when someone behaves like their parents or chooses the same careers as their parents. For example, ***Stephen wants to become a councilman. Like father, like son.*** Interestingly, there is the same expression in Chinese called 有其父必有其子. 父 means "father"; 子 means "son" in Chinese.

Like father, like son 為一個古老的諺語。它描述某人與其父母在外表及行為上極為相似。這句諺語通常在某人表現與父母類似的行為，或從事與父母相同的職業時使用。比方說，***Stephen 想要成為一位議員，有其父必有其子***。有趣的是，這與中文的成語─有其父必有其子不謀而同。

Synonyms and Analysis 中西諺語應用與翻譯

The original idiom 原來怎麼說

Like father, like son

Synonyms 還能怎麼翻

A chip off the old block, follow in someone's footsteps, be similar to, look like, take after, resemble, spitting image

Explanations 中西諺語翻譯說明

A chip off the old block is another way to express like father, like son. It indicates someone whose personality or appearance is similar to his or her parents. Following in someone's footsteps also has the similar meaning, but it indicates following someone's lifestyle or careers.

Spitting image expresses two persons look alike a lot. For example, ***Tom is the spitting image of his grandfather.*** You can also describe like father, like son in a simple way, such as be similar to, look like, take after, or resemble.

A chip off the old block 為另一個形容 like father, like son 的慣用語。它說明某人的個性、或外表與其父母相像。Following in someone's footsteps 有著類似的意思，但通常用來表示追隨他人的生活方式或職業。

Spitting image 表示長得非常像某人。舉例來說，***Tom 與其祖父長得一模一樣***。也可以用簡單的方式來形容 Like father, like son，如 be similar to、look like、take after 或者是 resemble。

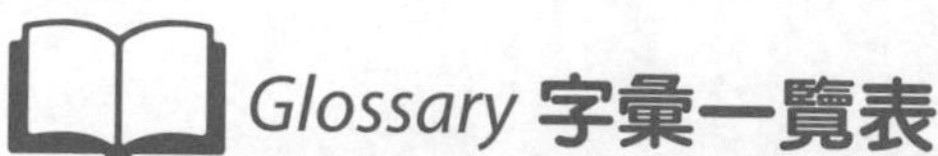

a chip off the old block *ph.* 在性格上與其父母的一方相似	**follow** *v.* 跟隨
lifestyle *n.* 生活方式	**career** *n.* 職業
spitting image *n.* 一模一樣的人或東西	**resemble** *v.* 類似
exactly *adv.* 完全地	**take after** *ph.* 相似

Analysis 中西諺語翻譯分析

Like father, like son and a chip off the old block are used as single phrases in sentences. For instance, ***Henry is very smart. I think he takes after his father's side of the family. Like father, like son. Richard looks exactly the same as his father, a chip off the old block.***

Both "look like" and "take after" are often used as phrasal verbs and put after subjects in sentences. An example can go like this: ***Jessica looked like her sister when she was small.***

Like father, like son 及 a chip off the old block 在句中作為單一片語使用。比方說，***Henry 好聰明，我認為他是遺傳了父親那邊。有其父必有其子。Richard 長得跟他的父親一模一樣。有其父必有其子。***

Look like 和 take after 通常於句子中置於主詞後，作為片語動詞使用。它們的應用為：***Jessica 和她姐姐小時候很相似。***

FAQ 中西文化外交交流的一問三答 Track 04

Q ***What is the difference between "like father, like son" and "follow in someone's footsteps"?***

***Like father, like son* 和 *follow in someone's footsteps* 有什麼差異之處？**

❶ Apparently, like father, like son describes a person who looks like or behaves like one of his parents.

很明顯的，Like father, like son 形容某人之行為舉止或外表像其父母之一方。

❷ To follow in someone's footsteps usually indicates following the same career or doing the same thing as someone else does.

To follow in someone's footsteps 通常指仿傚他人的職業或選擇。

❸ Like father, like son expresses that a son takes after his father but to follow in someone's footsteps can also describe doing the same thing as someone else does. They don't have to be fathers or mothers. They can be anyone, such as teachers or mentors.

Like father, like son 表示兒子像父親，但 to follow in someone's footsteps 可以用來形容和他人做一樣的事情。他人不一定是父母親，可以為任何人，像是老師或指導者。

Q How do you describe "spitting image" in Chinese?
如何用中文形容 Spitting image 呢？

❶ Well, it is similar to the expression "一模一樣" in Chinese. 模 and 樣 mean appearance in Chinese. So it means two or more things/ persons look exactly the same.

它和中文的一模一樣類似。模和樣在中文和英文的appearance相同，它的意思為兩個以上的是人、事或物長得簡直一樣。

❷ You can say 如出一轍. 轍 means the trace left by cars in Chinese. When two traces come from the same car, the traces will be no difference. This expression indicates someone's behaviour is the same as one of another person.

你可以說如出一轍。轍在中文意指車走過留下的軌跡。當兩道軌跡來自於同一個車輛時，那麼這兩道軌跡幾乎沒有不同。這樣的表達是用來形容像極了某人的行為。

❸ 簡直是一個模子刻出來的 is an interesting expression. 模子 is a mould and 刻, the act of carving. When you follow a mould to carve, you will get products looking exactly the same. It means two people look alike so much that it's like they are from the same mould.

簡直是一個模子刻出來的是一個有趣的表達方式。模子為 mould，而刻為 the act of carving。當你照著一個模子去刻，你會做出一模一樣的產品來。它表示長得和某人一模一樣。根本像是同一個模子刻出來的。

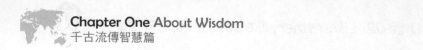

Q What are the antonyms of spitting image in Chinese?

Spitting image 的反義字為？

❶ Well, there are many ways to describe the antonyms of spitting image in Chinese, such as 截然不同. It means totally different.

有許多的方法可形容 Spitting image 的反義字，像是截然不同。它是指完全不一樣。

❷ You can also say 天淵之別. Its literal meaning is the distance between sky and ground is so far. It denotes a great difference.

你也可以說天淵之別。它字面上的意思為天與地的差距極遠，暗示著差異極大。

❸ Um, 大相徑庭 is a good example. It indicates two people who behave differently.

嗯，大相徑庭是一個好的例子。它指兩個人的行為差別很大。

Vocabulary 重點單字

- **resemble** *v.* 看起來像

例：Heather resembles her sister a lot. They look like twins.
Heather 看起來像極了她的姐姐。倆人好似雙胞胎。

- **councilman** *n.* 議員

例：He has been elected to become a councilman for the local government.
他被選為當地政府的一位議員。

- **personality** *n.* 個性

例：Her personality is very different from her brother's.
她的個性和她的哥哥非常不一樣。

- **appearance** *n.* 外表

例：I haven't seen Andy for a long time. His appearance has completely changed.
我很久沒看到 Andy 了。他的外表改變了很多。

- **footstep** *n.* 腳步

例：Steve heard the footsteps in the living room. He thought it was a thief.
Steve 聽到客廳的腳步聲。他以為那是小偷。

- **mentor** *n.* 指導者

例：When I joined the company, Sharon was my mentor.
當我加入公司時，Sharon 為我的指導者。

- **mould** *n.* 模子

例：My mother bought a jelly mould to make coffee jelly.
我的媽媽買了一個果凍模子作咖啡凍。

- **influence** *v.* 影響

例：Outgoing people are good at influencing their friends.
外向的人擅於影響他們的朋友。

文化巧巧說：諺語與外交相關的文化趣事

Both Chinese and English have the same expression to describe like father, like son. The idea of 有其父必有其子 is that sons are often influenced by their fathers. Therefore, they act and behave like their fathers. When people see their sons behave the same as their fathers, they usually say 有其父必有其子.

A chip off the old block is very close to like father, like son. The early description of this phrase is "chip of the same block". It appeared in Bishop (of Lincoln) Robert Sanderson's Sermons in the seventeenth century. Both like father, like son and a chip off the old block are in everyday use.

There are so many ways to describe like father, like son in English and Chinese. If you can learn and use its synonyms, it helps you not to repeat yourself in your conversations or writings.

中文和英文皆有一樣的表達方式來形容 Like father, like son。有其父必有其子的想法為兒子深受父親所影響。因此，他們的言行舉止與其父親一樣。當人們看見兒子表現與父親相同時，通常會有感而發說有其父必有其子。

A chip off the old block 與 like father, like son 十分相近。早期的說法為 Chip of the same block。它於十七世紀時出現於 Bishop (of Lincoln) Robert Sanderson's Sermons。Like father, like son 及 a chip off the old block 皆很實用。

中文和英文皆有很多方式來形容 Like father, like son。如果你能學習並活用它的同義字，這可以幫你避免於會話中重覆使用相同詞句的窘境。

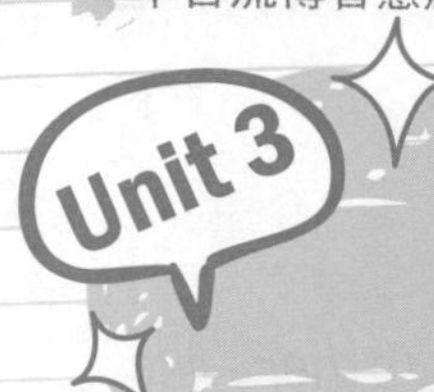

Unit 3 Look before you leap 三思而後行

How to use this idiom and on what occasions you can use this idiom 這句諺語你會怎麼說、能派上用場的場合

Track 05

Literally speaking, this proverb is used to advise someone to think carefully before they act. This proverb was first recorded in the sixteenth century to describe an unprepared marriage. It can be used when you want to advise someone to think about the consequences before they make decisions. For example, ***A: I am going to quit my job and start my own company. B: You have to work very hard and sacrifice your time with your family. Look before you leap.***

從字面上來看，這句諺語用來忠告他人三思而行。Look before you leap最早於十六世紀時記載，來描述一段未準備的婚姻。它可用來忠告他人在做任何決定前，仔細考量其後果。舉例來說，***A：我要辭去工作，並創立我的公司。B：你必須很努力工作，並且犧牲掉你和家人的時間。請三思而行。***

Synonyms and Analysis 中西諺語應用與翻譯

The original idiom 原來怎麼說

Look before you leap

Synonyms 還能怎麼翻

Think something over, mull something over, think something through, think about, ponder, consideration

Explanations 中西諺語翻譯說明

Apart from look before you leap, you can also say think something over, mull something over, think something through, think about and ponder. Mull something over is to think about something carefully for a long time. For example, ***I can't make a decision now. I want to go home and mull it over.***

"Ponder" is formal English. You usually see it in the newspaper. Compared with "think something over" and "mull something over", "look before you leap" is for important decisions, such as buying a house or starting a business.

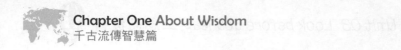

除了 Look before you leap 外，你也可以說 think something over、mull something over、think something through、think about、及 ponder。Mull something over 為仔細考量某事一段時間。比方說，***我無法現在做決定，我想回家並考慮一陣子。***

Ponder（思量）為正式的英文。通常於報紙上出現。與 Think something over 和 mull something over 比較，look before you leap 用於重大的決定，像是買屋或創業等。

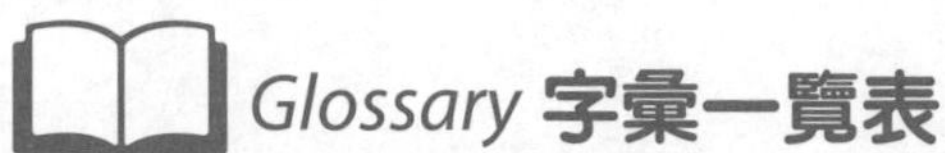

Glossary 字彙一覽表

leap *v.* 跳躍	**mull** *v.* 仔細考慮
compare with *ph.* 與……相比	**carefully** *adv.* 仔細地
formal *adj.* 正式的	**matter** *n.* 事情
possible *adj.* 可能的	**interview** *n.* 面試

Analysis 中西諺語翻譯分析

Look before you leap is usually used as a single phrase in sentences. For instance, ***before you borrow money from a bank, you should think how you can pay it back. Look before you leap.***

To think something over, mull something over, think something through and think about are used as phrasal verbs in sentences. Examples can go like this: ***Cindy just needs a few minutes to think this matter over. Think through all the possible questions before you have an interview.***

Look before you leap 通常於句子中作為單一片語使用。舉例來說，***在你向銀行借錢前，你應該先想該如何還錢。請三思而行。***

To think something over、mull something over、think something through 及 think about 在句子中作為片語動詞使用。舉例來說：***Cindy 只需要幾分鐘的時間來想這件事。於面試前，徹底地想清楚所有可能會問的問題。***

FAQ 中西文化外交交流的一問三答 Track 06

Q ***What are the differences among "looking before you leap", "to think something over" and "to ponder"?***

請問 *Look before you leap*、*think something over* 及 *ponder* 之間有什麼不同？

❶ Um, looking before you leap is used for something important and you have to think about its consequences.

嗯，look before you leap 為考量比較重要的事，而且要想到後果。

❷ Well, to think something over is usually used for small things, such as buying a dress.

Think something over 通常是指考量小事，像是買衣服。

❸ To ponder is formal and it is usually used in written English. To think something over is colloquial.

Ponder 為正式用法，它通常用於英文寫作。Think something over 為口語用法。

Q When do you use thinking something over, to mull something over and looking before you leap?
何種情況下可使用 Think something through、mull something over 及 look before you leap？

❶ You can use thinking something over and looking before you leap in daily conversation.

你可以用 Mull something over 及 look before you leap 於日常會話中。

❷ Well, thinking something over is to go through all the details before you make a decision. So it is for something relevant to work, studies, or important decisions.

Thinking something over 指在做決定前，仔細考量每個細節。因此，它與工作、學習或重要決策有關。

❸ Um, looking before you leap is used to advise someone to make a careful decision. Mulling something over is usually used to request for more time to think about something.

嗯，Looking before you leap 為用來勸他人小心做決定。Mulling something over 通常是用來要求更多的時間來考量。

Q ***Do you have any Chinese idioms similar to "look before you leap"?***

請問有其他的中文成語與 *Look before you leap* 相似嗎？

❶ Yes, we do. 三思而行 is a good example. It means think over many times before you act.

有的。三思而行是一個好的例子。它指做任何行動前，請多次衡量。

❷ 深思熟慮 is commonly used in conversation. It means to think carefully.

深思熟慮在會話中很常使用。它指仔細考慮。

❸ You can say 思前想後. Its meaning is to think repetitively. 前 means "front"; 後 "back" in Chinese. When someone looks front and back, it's like he or she is hesitating and cant't move on. It denotes thinking something over many times.

你可以說思前想後。它字面上的意思就是反覆思考。"Front" 和 "Back" 在中文裡是指前、後。當一個人思前想後，就表示這人正在猶豫，無法繼續下去，暗示再三思考。

Vocabulary 重點單字

- **sacrifice** *v.* 犧牲

  例：Lucy has sacrificed her dream job for her children.
  Lucy 為了她的孩子犧牲了她夢想的工作。

- **ponder** *v.* 仔細考量

  例：Wendy has been pondering her future but still can't make her mind up.
  Wendy 一直在考量她的未來，但是一直無法做決定。

- **consequence** *n.* 後果

  例：A wrong business decision will cause serious consequences.
  一個錯誤的商業決定會造成嚴重的後果。

- **possibility** *n.* 可能性

  例：There is a possibility of typhoon next week.
  下週可能會有颱風。

- **apart from** *prep.* 除了

  例：Apart from the piano, she can also play the violin.
  除了鋼琴外，她也會彈小提琴。

- **consideration** *n.* 考慮

  例：Your proposal is under consideration; please wait for a few days.
  你的提案目前正在考慮中，請等幾天的時間。

- **similarity** *n.* 相似點

  例：John and Peter are twins. Can you tell the similarities between John and Peter?
  John 和 Peter 為雙胞胎。你可以告訴我 John 和 Peter 的相似點嗎？

- **written** *adj.* 書面的

  例：This is not used in written English. It is used in spoken English.
  這個不是用於英文寫作上。它是用於英文口說。

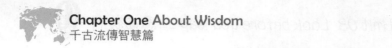

文化巧巧說：諺語與外交相關的文化趣事

Look before you leap is commonly used in the conversation to advise someone to think through different possibilities before making an important decision. This is similar to a Chinese idiom "三思而行".

Apart from 三思而行, you can also say 深思熟慮 or 遠慮深思. 深思熟慮 is the other Chinese idiom meaning thinking something over. 遠慮深思 means a careful consideration. It is formal and usually used in written Chinese. It is interesting to see so many similarities in both ancient Chinese and English phrases.

Look before you leap 常用於日常會話中，勸告他人在做重大決定前，反覆思量各種可能的狀況。這與中文的三思而行不謀而同。

除了三思而行外，你也可以說深思熟慮或遠慮深思。深思熟慮為另一個中文成語，意指認真考量。遠慮深思則表示深遠的思量。它較為正式且常用於中文書寫上。能看見古代中文及英文有這麼多的共通之處是十分有趣的。

Save one's bacon
及時營救

How to use this idiom and on what occasions you can use this idiom
這句諺語你會怎麼說、能派上用場的場合

Track 07

Save one's bacon is to avoid someone getting injured or getting into a difficult or dangerous situation. It is also called save one's neck or save one's skin. You can use this idiom when you get into trouble and someone turns up to help you. This idiom is close to Chinese phrases -及時營救 (help others' instantly) and 避免不幸 (avoid bad things from happening).

Save one's bacon 為形容避免某人受傷，或陷入一個困境。它也可以稱作 save one's neck 或 save one's skin。你可以在你遇到了一個麻煩，而某位人士出手相救時，使用這個諺語。這句諺語也與中文慣用語 - 及時營救及避免不幸類似。

Synonyms and Analysis 中西諺語應用與翻譯

The original idiom 原來怎麼說

Save one's bacon

Synonyms 還能怎麼翻

Save someone's life, save someone in the nick of time, save one's skin, save one's neck

Explanations 中西諺語翻譯說明

Another common phrase to describe this situation is saving someone's life. Literally speaking, saving someone's life indicates preventing someone from dying. For example, ***my operation went successfully; the doctor saved my life.*** It also means to help someone escaping from a difficult situation. For instance, ***thank you for keeping the secret. You really saved my life.***

To save someone in the nick of time is an expression describing someone has been saved at the last moment. For example, ***the ambulance arrived just in time. His life was saved in the nick of time.***

另一個常用的慣用語為 Save someone's life。就字面上的意思，Save someone' s life 指救了某人一命。比如說，***我的手術很成功，醫生救了我一命。它也指幫助某人脫離一個困境。舉例來說，謝謝你幫我保留秘密，你真的救了我一命。***

Save someone in the nick of time 為表示某人在最後一刻時 被營救。比如說，***救護車即時趕到，他的性命也在最後一刻時被營救。***

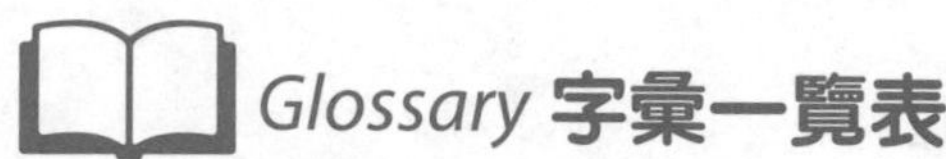

Glossary 字彙一覽表

operation *n.* 手術	**successfully** *adv.* 成功地
escape *v.* 逃離	**keep a secret** *ph.* 保守秘密
just in time *ph.* 及時	**in addition to** *conj.* 除了……之外
relative pronoun *n.* 關係代名詞	**police officer** *n.* 警員

Analysis 中西諺語翻譯分析

In addition to save one's bacon, you can also say "save one's skin" or "save one's neck". These phrases can be put after subjects. It can go like this: ***Joanne had a car accident last week. The airbag saved her bacon.*** You can also put it after relative pronouns. *It can go like this:* ***I went lost and couldn't find my way home. Luckily, I bumped into a police officer who saved my bacon.***

除了 Save one's bacon，你也可以用 Save one's skin 或 Save one's neck。這些諺語可以放在主詞之後，它的應用為：***Joanne 上週發生車禍。安全氣袋救了她一命。***

你也可以將它放在關係代名詞之後，比如說：***我走失了，找不到回家的路。很幸運地，我遇到了一名警察，他救了我一命。***

FAQ 中西文化外交交流的一問三答 Track 08

Q **_Why did this idiom use bacon?_**
為什麼這個諺語用 _Bacon_？

❶ Bacon didn't mean the back of a pig in the past. It could mean any part of the animal. To save your bacon means to save your body from getting injured.

Bacon 在過去並不是指豬的背部。它是指動物身體的任何一個部分。Save your bacon 意指避免身體部分受到傷害。

❷ Well, it is an interesting point. It didn't really mean pork at that time. That's why people also call it "save one's neck" and "save one's skin".

嗯，這是個有趣的點。它當時並不是指豬肉。這也是它又稱作 "save one's neck" 及 "save one's skin" 的原因。

❸ The origin of this idiom doesn't refer to bacon nowadays. It simply means the human body.

這個諺語的起源並不是指現在的培根喔。它是指身體的部分。

Q What are the differences between "save one's bacon" and "save someone in the nick of time"? "Save one's bacon" 及 "save someone in the nick of time" 有什麼不同？

❶ As you can see from the original phrase, it adds "in the nick of time" in the end of the phrase. "In the nick of time" indicates just in time. So it means save someone just in time.

由原本的諺語可見，它在句子後面加入了 in the nick of time。In the nick of time 是指及時的意思。所以整句為及時救了某人一命的意思。

❷ Well, they are very similar. To save someone in the nick of time means someone's help arrived at the last minute.

嗯，它們十分的相似。Save someone in the nick of time 指救兵及時趕到的意思。

❸ "In the nick of time" is another idiom describing the last moment. So "Save someone in the nick of time" means saving someone at the last moment.

"In the nick of time" 為另一個諺語，指最後一刻的意思。所以 Save someone in the nick of time 指在最後一刻及時趕到。

Q When do you use "save one's bacon"?
何時使用 Save one's bacon？

❶ You can use "save one's bacon" when you just have escaped from a dangerous or a difficult situation.

當你剛從一個危險的困境中掙脫出來時，你可以用 "save one's bacon" 來形容。

❷ Well, my friend has just said "You saved my bacon" yesterday because I lent him some money to pay his rent.

嗯，我的朋友昨天剛跟我說：「你救了我一命。」，因為我借錢給他，幫他付租金。

❸ When you have just been rescued and want to appreciate someone's help, you can say "Thank you. You saved my bacon".

當你剛剛被救出，且想要向對方道謝時，你可以說：「謝謝你，你救了我一命。」。

Vocabulary 重點單字

- **injury** *n.* 受傷

例：Judy was so lucky to escape from an earthquake without injury.
Judy 十分幸運地逃離一場地震，並且沒有受傷。

- **prevent from** *ph.* 阻止；預防

例：Cindy tried to prevent her boyfriend from running away but it didn't work.
Cindy 試著阻止其男友變心，但是不成功。

- **ambulance** *n.* 救護車

例：Cars should give ways to ambulances.
汽車應該讓路給救護車。

- **airbag** *n.* 安全氣袋

例：An airbag is an essential safety equipment for car drivers.
安全氣袋對於汽車駕駛而言，為必要的安全設施。

- **bump into** *v.* 巧遇

例：What a coincidence! I bumped into an old classmate today.
好巧啊！我今天遇到了一位舊同學。

- **poem** *n.* 詩

例：This poet wrote many beautiful poems and published his book.
這位詩人寫了所多首美麗的詩，並將其出版成書。

- **Song Dynasty** *n.* 宋朝

例：The history museum is exhibiting many old paintings from the Song Dynasty.
歷史博物館目前在展宋朝時的舊畫。

文化巧巧說：諺語與外交相關的文化趣事

Bacon didn't not mean meat from the back of a pig in the olden days. It does not indicate a specific part of meat. "Save your bacon" simply denotes preventing from getting injured. This idiom appeared in an article in the seventeenth century. It has been widely used in daily conversation.

The relevant Chinese phrases are 及時營救 and 避免不幸. They mean you saved someone's life by helping someone in the nick of time. You can simply say 救某人一命 to indicate saving someone's life. 及時雨 has similar meaning to save one's bacon. Literally speaking it indicates a rain comes just in time but it implies something you need comes just in time. This phrase appeared in a poem in the Song Dynasty but it has been widely used nowadays.

A similar phrase called "save your own skin" has a different meaning. It means you only protect yourself in a dangerous situation and neglect other people. It is totally different from "save one's bacon". Don't mix them up.

Bacon 在過去並不是指豬的背部。但它並沒有明確指出特定的部位。Save your bacon 其實就是指避免某人受傷的意思。這個諺語在十七世紀時出現在一個文章裡。它已被廣泛地運用在日常對話裡。

相關的中文慣用語包括及時營救及避免不幸。它們指及時拯救了某人。你也可以說"救某人一命"來表達相同的意思。及時雨與 save one's bacon 也有相似之處。從字面上來看，它指一場大雨來的正好，但意指所需的事物及時到來。這個慣用語在中國宋朝的詩句中出現，至今已被廣泛地使用。

另一個相似諺語 – Save your own skin 有不同的意思。它指在危險的情勢中，你只顧著你自身的安全，而忽視他人。這與 save one's bacon 不同，不要搞混了。

As busy as a bee
忙得不可開交

How to use this idiom and on what occasions you can use this idiom
這句諺語你會怎麼說、能派上用場的場合

Track 09

Literally speaking, as busy as a bee uses a bee as an example to describe someone is very busy. This phrase derives from Chaucer's *Canterbury Tales* in the fourteenth century. It is commonly used to describe someone who is very busy and doing many things. For example, ***Linda is a single parent. She is as busy as a bee, always looking after her children and doing housework.*** This is similar to a Chinese phrase - 忙得不可開交; in Chinese, 開交 means something is twisted so tightly that it's not easy to break it off.

從字面上來看，as busy as a bee 以蜜蜂作為例子來形容某人十分地忙碌。它源自於十四世紀喬叟的《坎特伯利集》。As busy as a bee 被廣泛地用來形容同時做很多事，非常繁忙的樣子。舉例來說，***Linda 為單親媽媽，她總是忙碌地照顧孩子及做家事***。這也與中文的忙得不可開交不謀而同。開交指得是兩者交纏緊密不易斷開的意思。

Synonyms and Analysis 中西諺語應用與翻譯

The original idiom 原來怎麼說

as busy as a bee

Synonyms 還能怎麼翻

Busy, active, engaged, on the go, snowed under

Explanations 中西諺語翻譯說明

Snowed under is another way to describe as busy as a bee. If someone is snowed under, it means that he or she is very busy. For example, ***I'm afraid that Lucy is not available now. She is snowed under with work.*** You can also express as busy as a bee in a simple way, such as busy, active and engaged.

Snowed under 為另一個形容 as busy as a bee 的方法。假如某人為 snowed under，這代表他十分地忙碌。比如說，***我很抱歉 Lucy 現在沒空，她目前工作很忙***。也可以用簡單的方式來形容 as busy as a bee，像是 busy, active 或 engaged。

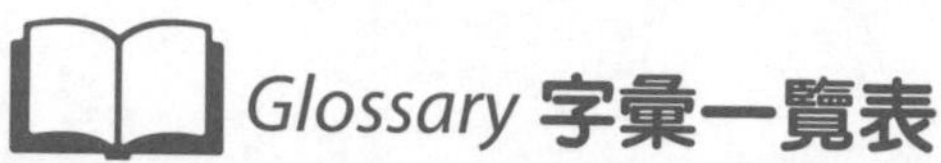

Glossary 字彙一覽表

active *adj.* 忙碌的；活躍的	**on the go** *ph.* 忙個不停的
snow under *ph.* 忙不過來	**afraid** *adj.* 很遺憾；抱歉
available *adj.* 有空的	**start a new business** *ph.* 創立新企業

Analysis 中西諺語翻譯分析

Snowed under is usually put after verbs in sentences. An example can go like this: ***Nick is snowed under today.*** Engaged usually comes with "in". For instance, ***Sarah is engaged in her new job.***

On the go is put after verbs in sentences. For example, ***Johnny has been on the go since he started his new business.***

Snowed under 通常於句子中放在動詞後使用。它的應用為：***Nick 今天有好幾件事要辦***。Engaged 通常會隨著"in"來使用。舉例來說，***Sarah 目前正忙著她的新工作***。On the go 一般放在動詞後使用。比如說，***Johnny 自從創業後，就一直忙個不停***。

Notes

FAQ 中西文化外交交流的一問三答 Track 10

Q ***I heard there are many phrases using as …as…. Do you know any phrases using as…as…?***

我聽說有許多的慣用語使用 *as …as…*，請問有哪些慣用語用 *as …as…*？

❶ As red as a lobster is a good example. You can easily guess its meaning. It indicates sunburnt skin.

As red as a lobster 是一個好的例子。你可以輕易地猜出它的意思來。它指日曬後的皮膚。

❷ Well, I know as bald as a coot. It means no hair.

我知道 As bald as a coot。它意指無髮。

❸ As cool as a cucumber indicates someone who is very calm. It is an interesting expression, isn't it?

As cool as a cucumber 表示某人非常地冷靜。這是個有趣的表達方式，不是嗎？

Q As...as...expressions sound interesting. Can you give me more examples?

As...as...的詞句十分地有趣，請問你可以舉更多的例子嗎？

❶ For as red as a lobster, you can say "I'll be as red as a lobster when I come back from Thailand."

對於 as red as a lobster，你可以說：「我從泰國回來後，會曬得通紅」。

❷ Here is an example. One of my uncles was very handsome when he was young but he is as bald as a coot now.

這裡有個例子。我的一位叔叔年輕時很英俊，但現在變禿子了。

❸ For as cool as a cucumber, an example can go like this: I'm shocked he was as cool as a cucumber. He is usually a nervous person.

對於 as cool as a cucumber，它的例子為：我很驚訝他如此冷靜。他平時是個緊張的人。

Q Do you have similar phrases in Chinese?

請問中文中有任何類似 *as busy as a bee* 的慣用語嗎？

❶ Yes, you can say 忙得不可開交. It means that there are so many things to do and you don't have time to take a rest. This phrase is commonly used in Chinese.

有喔，你可以說忙得不可開交。它意指有好幾件事要辦，忙得沒有時間休息。這句慣用語在中文很常使用。

❷ 忙不過來 is colloquial. It means too busy to finish your work.

忙不過來很口語喔。它指忙到沒有時間完成手邊的工作。

❸ 慌慌忙忙 is slightly different from the previous examples. It means very busy and nervous.

慌慌忙忙跟前面的例子較不同。它表示非常忙碌及緊張。

Vocabulary 重點單字

- **engaged** *adj.* 忙於

  例：Sean is engaged in expanding factories now.
  Sean 正忙著工廠擴展的工作。

- **suntanned** *adj.* 日曬後皮膚曬成棕色的

  例：After a trip to Dubai, my friend had suntanned skin.
  我的朋友去一趟杜拜後，皮膚曬成棕色的。

- **as red as a lobster** *ph.* 皮膚曬成通紅

  例：She will be as red as a lobster after the summer.
  她在夏天後，膚色會曬成通紅的。

- **as bald as a coot** *ph.* 全禿的

  例：If you keep going out on rainy days without an umbrella, you will be as bald as a coot.
  如果你一直在下雨天出門不帶傘，你會頭頂全禿的。

- **as cool as a cucumber** *ph.* 冷靜的

  例：Jessica is always as cool as a cucumber even if she loses her wallet.
  Jessica 總是十分冷靜，即使是她丟了錢包。

- **disorder** *n.* 混亂

  例：His wife was on a business trip for a week. The whole house was in disorder.
  他的太太出差一週。整個家很亂。

- **unlikely** *adj.* 不太可能的

  例：It is very sunny today. It is unlikely to rain.
  天氣這麼晴朗，今天不太可能會下雨。

文化巧巧說：諺語與外交相關的文化趣事

As busy as a bee uses "bee" in the figurative sense because people think bees are usually busy with their work. Snowed under is also used with a more imaginative meaning. It denotes that there are many things to do at the same time.

There are many Chinese phrases describing very busy, such as 忙得不可開交, 忙不過來, 忙忙碌碌, 忙手忙腳 or 忙上加忙. They are similar to each other but can be described in different situations. 忙不過來 means there are too many things and it is unlikely to finish all of them. The literal meaning of 忙手忙腳 is busy hands and busy feet. It indicates it is very busy and everything is in disorder. 忙上加忙 means that it is getting busier and busier. If you are 忙上加忙, it means that you are getting more work to do and it makes you busier. It is interesting that there are so many ways to express busy in different situations.

There are many English phrases using animals or foods as examples, such as "as red as a lobster", "as bald as a coot" and "as cool as a cucumber". It is interesting to see these phrases are used with imaginative meanings. It also helps people to memorize them easily and use them in daily conversation.

由於一般人認為蜜蜂時常辛勤地工作，所以 as busy as a bee 使用蜜蜂來比喻。Snowed under 也是用具有想像力的方式來形容。它表示同時要做好幾件事。

有許多中文慣用語描述非常忙碌，像是忙得不可開交、忙不過來、忙忙碌碌、忙手忙腳、或是忙上加忙。它們雖然相似，但是用於形容不同的情況。忙不過來指有太多事要做，可能無法全部完成。忙手忙腳的字面意思為忙碌的手腳。它意指非常忙亂。忙上加忙指愈來愈忙。假如你處於忙上加忙的情況，它表示你有愈來愈多的工作要做，這使你更加地忙碌。有許多方式來形容忙碌的情形是十分地有趣。

有許多的英文慣用語使用動物及食物來舉例，像是"as red as a lobster"，"as bald as a coot" 及"as cool as a cucumber"。這些慣用語使用具有想像空間的形容法，非常有趣。它也幫助人們輕鬆記憶，並活用於日常會話中。

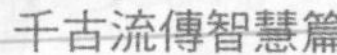

Speak of the devil 說到曹操，曹操就到

How to use this idiom and on what occasions you can use this idiom 這句諺語你會怎麼說、能派上用場的場合

Track 11

When someone you are talking about arrives unexpectedly, you can use this expression to describe this situation. This idiom is commonly used in any occasion. You can also call it "talk of the devil". For instance, ***A: Judy went travelling last month. I haven't seen her for a long time. B: Speak of the devil, here she comes.*** Speak of the devil appeared in the sixteenth century in old English texts. 說到曹操，曹操就到 is the Chinese version of ***"speak of the devil".***

當你在談論的某人突然無預警地出現時，你可以用此句來敘述這個情況。這個諺語廣泛地被應用於任何的場合。它也可稱為 Talk of the devil。舉例來說，***A：Judy上個月去旅行後，我已經很久沒有看見她了。B：說到曹操，曹操就到，她來了***。Speak of the devil 為十六世紀時出現在英文古文。說到曹操，曹操就到則是中文版的 speak of the devil。

Synonyms and Analysis 中西諺語應用與翻譯

The original idiom 原來怎麼說

speak of the devil

Synonyms 還能怎麼翻

Talk of the devil, speak of the devil and he will appear, what a coincidence

Explanations 中西諺語翻譯說明

The full sentence of this idiom is "speak of the devil and he will appear". The other similar way to describe this idiom is what a coincidence! For example, ***what a coincidence! I've just thought about you and you rang.*** What a coincidence is also very similar to Chinese idioms - 無巧不成書 or 無巧不成話。無巧不成話 means that if there is no coincidence, it would not become a story people talk about.

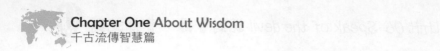

這個諺語的原句為 speak of the devil and he will appear。其他相似的形容法為 What a coincidence；比如說：***好巧喔！我正在想你，你就打電話來了***。What a coincidence 也與中文的諺語 - 無巧不成書或無巧不成話相似。無巧不成話指的是如果不是巧合，它就不會成為一個眾人討論的故事。

Glossary 字彙一覽表

appear *v.* 出現	**what a coincidence** *ph.* 好巧喔
ring *v.* 打電話	**emphasize** *v.* 強調
unplanned *adj.* 未計畫的	**apartment** *n.* 公寓
colleague n. 同事	

Analysis 中西諺語翻譯分析

"Speak of the devil" and "talk of the devil" can be put in end of the sentence when you mention someone appears. It can go like this: ***We just talked about you. Speak of the devil and you came.*** "What a coincidence" can be put in the beginning of the sentence when you want to emphasize this unplanned situation. It can go like: ***What a coincidence. We moved in to an apartment next to my colleague's.***

Speak of the devil 及 talk of the devil 可以放在句子的後面來提及某人突然出現。它的應用為：***我們剛剛在說你，說到曹操，曹操就到，你出現了***。當你想強調一件不預期的事時，what a coincidence 可放在句子的開頭。它的應用為：***好巧喔。我們搬到我同事附近的公寓***。

Notes

FAQ 中西文化外交交流的一問三答 Track 12

Q ***Why is this idiom related to the devil?***
為什麼這個諺語與 *Devil* 有關？

❶ Well, it was a superstitious belief that it is prohibited to talk about the devil directly.

嗯，這是當時迷信的想法，人們為禁止直接提到惡魔（devil）。

❷ It is a religious thing. People didn't talk about the devil in public in the olden days because they worried the devil would appear.

這與宗教有關。在過去，民眾不在公眾場合提到惡魔（devil），因為他們擔心惡魔會出現。

❸ The original idiom is "speak of the devil and he will appear". As you can see from this idiom, people worry that the devil will turn up if they talk about him.

原本的諺語為 Speak of the devil and he will appear. 由此可見，人們擔心講到惡魔後，它會現身。

Q Do you use both "talk of the devil" and "speak of the devil"?

Talk of the devil 及 Speak of the devil 你兩個都用嗎？

❶ Yes, you can say either "talk of the devil" or "speak of the devil".

可以，你可以說 speak of the devil 或 talk of the devil.

❷ Yes, we do. "Talk of the devil" was first recorded in an old English book in the sixteenth century and "speak of the devil" is commonly used nowadays.

是的，我們可以。Talk of the devil 最先被記錄在一本十六世紀時的英文書，而 speak of the devil 則較被廣泛地運用。

❸ Yes, we do. Apart from "talk of the devil" and "speak of the devil", you can also say "Speak of the devil and in he walks" and "Speak of the devil and he is sure to appear".

是的，除了 Talk of the devil 及 Speak of the devil 外，你也可以說 Speak of the devil and in he walks 及 Speak of the devil and he is sure to appear。

Q Do you have similar idioms in Chinese?
你們有任何類似的中文成語嗎？

❶ Yes, we do. 說到曹操，曹操就到 and 無巧不成書 are commonly used in daily conversation.

是的，我們有。說到曹操，曹操就到及無巧不成書很常使用到。

❷ 說到曹操，曹操就到 is an ancient Chinese story describing 曹操 appearing unexpectedly when you talked about him.

說到曹操，曹操就到來自於一個古老的中國故事，形容在談及曹操時，他無預警的現身。

❸ 無巧不成書 indicates an unplanned event that happens by coincidence.

無巧不成書指發生的一個巧合。

Vocabulary 重點單字

- **unexpectedly** *adv.* 未料到地

例：The president turned up unexpectedly. You have to pick him up at the airport.
總經理突然到來。你必須到機場接他。

- **coincidence** *n.* 巧合

例：This is a coincidence that Judy and Vivian chose the same name for their daughters.
Judy 和 Vivian 為她們的女兒取相同的名字為巧合。

- **devil** *n.* 惡魔

例：Sam had a car accident and had been in the hospital in the last two weeks. Oh, poor devil.
Sam 發生車禍，並待在醫院兩週。喔，好可憐。

- **superstitious** *adj.* 迷信的

例：Some people are superstitious and believe that number four is unlucky.
有些人十分迷信，並相信數字四不吉利。

- **belief** *n.* 信仰

例：Different religious beliefs bring different life styles.
不同的宗教信仰有著不同的生活習慣。

- **prohibit** *v.* 禁止

例：Gambling is strictly prohibited in this area.
賭博在這個區域是被禁止的。

- **origin** *n.* 起源

例：What is the origin of this story? Its origin is obscure.
這個故事的起源為何？它的來源為鮮為人知的。

- **mix something/ somebody up** *ph.* 弄混

例：Nick and Gary are twins. People often mix them up.
Nick 和 Gary 為雙胞胎。人們常常把他們搞混。

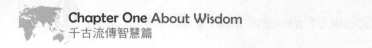

文化巧巧說：諺語與外交相關的文化趣事

This phrase was originally from England and first printed in the sixteenth century. Although the English idiom – Speaking of the devil and the Chinese idiom - 說到曹操，曹操就到 have different origins, they indicate the same meaning.

Another similar idiom called speaking of which. When you mention something in your conversation, you can use this phrase to refer to something in the previous conversation. It is very similar to by the way. For example, ***it looks like it is going to rain soon. Speaking of which, have you bought an umbrella?***

These two idioms are similar but they are used in different situations. Try to practice them with your friends and do not mix them up.

這個諺語原本來自於英國，並於十六世紀首次發行。雖然英文諺語 speaking of the devil 及中文成語 – 說到曹操，曹操就到有著不同的起源，但他們有著一樣的意思。

另一個類似的諺語為 Speaking of which（講到這個）。當你在會話中提及某事，你可用此慣用語作為連接上一句的轉換詞。它與 By the way 十分的相似。舉例來說，看起來快下雨了。講到這個，你有帶雨傘嗎？

這兩個諺語十分地類似，但它們是使用在不同的情況。試著與你的朋友互相練習，別將這兩句搞混了喔！

At the drop of a hat
毫不猶豫

How to use this idiom and on what occasions you can use this idiom
這句諺語你會怎麼說、能派上用場的場合

Track 13

When you do something at the drop of a hat, you do it immediately without any hesitation or preparation. You use this phrase when you try to emphasise you could stop what you are currently doing and concentrating on doing another thing immediately. For instance, ***if I haven't been home for five years and I miss home very much, I could pack my luggage and go home at the drop of a hat.*** One the other hand, you could use this idiom when you want to emphasise you could do something easily and quickly. For example, ***David hates doing sit-ups but Ben could do them at the drop of a hat.***

當你毫不猶豫地做某事時，你會不加思索及毫無準備地立刻做此事。當你想強調你可以放下手邊的事情，立即去做某一件事時，可使用這個諺語。舉例來說，***假使我五年沒回家，而且我十分地思念家鄉，我會毫不猶豫地打包行李回家***。另一方面，你也可以使用這個諺語形容你可以快速及簡單地做某事。舉例來說，***David 討厭做仰臥起坐，Ben 可以不加思索的做***。

Synonyms and Analysis 中西諺語應用與翻譯

The original idiom 原來怎麼說

At the drop of a hat

Synonyms 還能怎麼翻

At once, straight away, immediately, promptly, instantly

Explanations 中西諺語翻譯說明

The other way to describe this idiom is doing something without hesitation, at once, immediately, instantly and so on. For example, ***I could sign this contract without hesitation because I have been waiting for this project.*** If you are familiar with a job and can easily finish it, you could use this phrase in this situation. For example, ***Gary is an experienced technician. He could fix the problem at the drop of a hat.***

This could be used with another idiom called "a piece of cake". It means that something is so easy and you can finish it quickly. You can describe this task as a piece of cake. For instance, ***A: This project's deadline is tomorrow. Will you be able to deliver it on time? B: A piece of cake.***

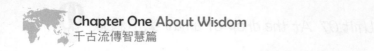

其他形容這句諺語的方法為毫不遲疑地做某事、立即、馬上等等。例如，***我已經等這個案子很久了，我可以毫不遲疑地簽這個合約***。假如你對某個工作十分熟悉，並可輕易地完成它，你也可以使用這個諺語在句子中。比如說，**Gary 為一位有經驗的技術人員。他可以立即處理好這個問題**。

這也可與另一個諺語 - A piece of cake 用。它指一件簡單及可輕易完成的事。你可以用來形容一件任務為容易的事。例如，***A：這個專案的交期為明天。你有辦法如期完成嗎？B：非常容易的事***。

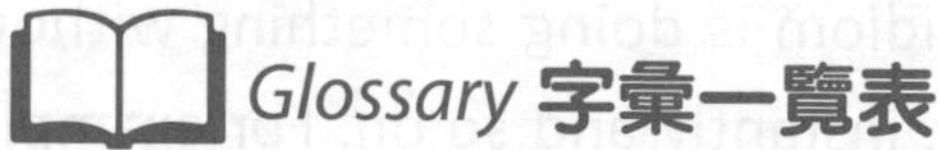

Glossary 字彙一覽表

at once *adv.* 馬上	**straight away** *adv.* 立即
promptly *adv.* 立即地	**be familiar with** *ph.* 對……熟悉
technician *n.* 技師	**a piece of cake** *ph.* 容易的事
earthquake *n.* 地震	**elevator** *n.* 電梯

Analysis 中西諺語翻譯分析

At the drop of a hat can be used as a single phrase in sentences. Its synonyms - *immediately, promptly* and *instantly* are used as adverbs in sentences. *It can go like this:* ***If there is an earthquake, stop using elevators immediately.***

At the drop of a hat 在句子中作為單一片語。它的同義字 *immediately, promptly* 及 *instantly*，在句子中作為副詞。它的應用為：***假如遇到地震，請立即停止使用電梯***。

Notes

FAQ 中西文化外交交流的一問三答 Track 14

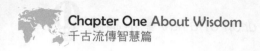

Q ***Why is a hat relevant to this idiom?***

為什麼帽子與這句諺語有關？

❶ Well, I know dropping a hat indicates a race was about to begin in the olden days.

嗯，我知道丟下帽子在過去為指示一場比賽的開始。

❷ Its origin was obscure but the most credible one is that hats were used to make signals in the past.

它的起源較鮮為人知的，但較可信的說法為帽子在過去為作為信號。

❸ At the drop of a hat derives from an old custom in the past. Dropping a hat signals a competition is ready to start, especially in a fight.

At the drop of a hat 是由過去的一個舊習俗來的。丟下帽子意指 一場比賽即將開始，特別是指打鬥。

Q How do you use this idiom in daily conversation?
如何在日常生活中運用這句諺語呢？

❶ Well, this idiom has multiple definitions. You can use it when you try to do something immediately. You can also use it when you try to say something can be done easily and quickly.

嗯，這句諺語有多個解釋喔。你可以用來說馬上做某事。你也可以用來說某事是可輕易且快速地被完成。

❷ Let me show you an example. My wife likes buying a lot of skin care products at the drop of a hat even though they are not useful.

讓我舉一個例子。我的太太喜歡買大量的保養品，即使它們一點也不實用。

❸ This idiom is very useful. I often use it when I try to say I can do something quickly. For example, my brother hates math but I can do it at the drop of a hat.

這個諺語非常的實用。我通常用它來形容我可以快速地做某事。比如說，我的弟弟討厭數學，但我可以不加思索的做。

Q Can you give me more examples about this idiom?
請問你可以舉更多關於這個諺語的例子嗎？

❶ Sure, here is an example. If I win a lottery, I could quit my job at the drop of a hat.

當然，這裡有個例子。假如我中了彩券，我可以不加思索地辭掉工作。

❷ As you know, at the drop of a hat also means doing something easily without any preparation. You can say "I am a highly skilled professional and have been doing the same job for many years. I can do it *at the drop of a hat* even though I am in a different country."

如你所知， at the drop of a hat 指可在毫無準備下做某件事。你可以說：「我是高技術的專業人士，且從事這個工作多年。我可以在毫無準備下做這個工作，即使是在不同的國家也是。」。

❸ Let me tell you my friend's example. Sue really wants to work overseas. If she gets a working holiday visa, she could set off *at the drop of a hat*.

讓我告訴你我朋友的例子。Sue 真的很想在海外工作。假如她取得打工渡假簽證，她可以立即出發。

Vocabulary 重點單字

- **hesitation** *n.* 猶豫

例：Emma agrees to lend her best friend money without any hesitation.
Emma 毫不遲疑地同意借錢給她最好的朋友。

- **concentrate on** *v.* 專心於

例：David failed his exam last semester. He must concentrate on his study now.
David 在上一個學期考試不及格。他現在可要好好地準備學習。

- **sit-ups** *n.* 仰臥起坐

例：Linda doesn't have time to go to a gym but she does sit-ups at home.
Linda 沒有時間去健身房，但她在家中做仰臥起坐。

- **multiple** *adj.* 多種的

例：Smart phones have multiple purposes nowadays.
現今智慧型手機有多種的用途。

- **working holiday visa** *n.* 打工渡假簽證

例：More and more young people are planning to apply for working holiday visas before they reach thirty years old.
愈來愈多的年輕人準備步入三十前，申請打工渡假簽證。

- **context** *n.* 上下文

例：This word has multiple definitions, it is better to check its context to understand its meaning.
這個字有多種的解釋。最好是看過它的上下文，再來解它的意思。

- **skilled professional** *n.* 高技能專業人士

例：Hannah is a high skilled professional. She can easily get a job she wants.
Hannah 為高技能專業人士，她可輕鬆地找到她想做的工作。

文化巧巧說：諺語與外交相關的文化趣事

As mentioned before, at the drop of a hat has multiple definitions. You can tell its meaning from its context. It can also be used in a situation when one can do something immediately without careful consideration. For instance, ***Maggie really likes designer's handbags. She can buy many handbags at the drop of a hat without thinking if she can afford them.***

When you talk about something that can be done easily without preparation, it is close to Chinese idioms 輕而易舉 and 易如反掌. It is often used in making contrasts in the following context. For example, ***I can't do math but my wife can do it at the drop of a hat.*** It is also often used with an English idiom "A piece of a cake". This is a way to show similarity in both cultures when you talk to English speakers.

如前面所述，at the drop of a hat 有多種的解釋。你可以藉由理解上下文來辨別它的意思。它也可以用來形容在沒有詳細的考量下，就立即決定做某事。舉例來説，Maggie 很喜愛名牌皮包，她可以在不考量是否能負擔的情況下，毫不猶豫地買了好幾個名牌皮包。

當你想提及一些可以輕鬆完成且不需準備的事時，這與中文成語－輕而易舉及易如反掌相似。它通常用在對比的情況。舉例來説，我無法計算，但我的太太可以輕而易舉的完成。它也與英文的諺語 a piece of a cake 相近。在與外籍人士對話時，也可以提及彼此文化的相似之處。

Below the belt
暗箭傷人

How to use this idiom and on what occasions you can use this idiom
這句諺語你會怎麼說、能派上用場的場合

Track 15

Below the belt was originally derived from boxing. It indicates hitting the opponent below the belt, which is unfair and against the rules. It is usually used with "hit". This idiom has been used widely nowadays to indicate unfair and dishonest behaviour. It is relevant to a Chinese idiom called 暗箭傷人. It means that achieving a goal by doing something sneaky or in an unscrupulous way.

Below the belt 原本是從拳擊延伸而來的。它意指打擊對手腰部以下，這是不公平且犯規的行為。Below the belt 通常與 hit 並用。這個諺語已被廣泛地運用來形容一些不公平及不誠實的行為。這與中文成語 - 暗箭傷人相似。這句成語指的是為達目的，在暗地裡做些不道德的事。

Synonyms and Analysis 中西諺語應用與翻譯

The original idiom 原來怎麼說

Below the belt

Synonyms 還能怎麼翻

Unfair, dishonest, unscrupulous, foul

Explanations 中西諺語翻譯說明

The other way to describe this idiom is dishonest conduct. Generally, it is used to criticise rivals' aggressive actions in business. For example, ***our competitor's marketing campaign hits below the belt and affects our sales significantly.***

A foul is another expression to describe an unfair act in a game or sport. It is usually used as a noun. For instance, ***a football player has committed a foul in a game.***

The examples above describe an action or behaviour. If you want to describe a dishonest person, you can use "twister". It is mainly used in Britain to describe someone who is double-dealing. For example, ***David always says bad things behind someone's back. He is a twister. However, it is informal and more colloquial in British English.***

其它形容這句諺語的形容詞像是 dishonest conduct。一般來說，它是用在批評競爭對手的激烈的商業競爭行為。舉例來說，***競爭對手的行銷活動暗地裡重重地打擊了我們的生意***。

Foul 為表達在比賽或運動中不公平的行為。它通常作為名詞，比如說，***這個足球選手在這次比賽中犯規***。

以上的例子為用來形容一種行動或行為。*若你想要形容一個不誠實的人，你可以用"twister"來表達。它主要用在英國來形容玩兩面手法的人。舉例來說*，***David 總是在背地裡說三道四，他是一個"Twister"***。然而，這個字較不正式且常用在口語的英式英文。

Notes

Analysis 中西諺語翻譯分析

Below the belt is used as a single phrase in sentences. Its synonyms - *unfair, dishonest* and *unscrupulous* are used as adjectives in sentences. An exampul can go like this: ***Cheating is a dishonest method in exams.***

Below the belt 在句子中做為單一片語使用。它的同義字 - *unfair, dishonest* 以及 *unscrupulous* 做為形容詞使用。相關的應用為：***作弊在考試中為一種不誠實的行為***。

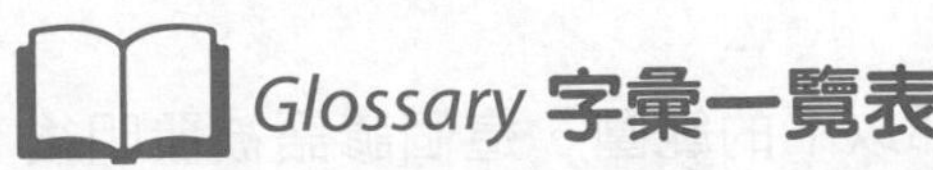

Glossary 字彙一覽表

a chip off the old block *ph.* 在性格上與其父母的一方相似	**follow** *v.* 跟隨
lifestyle *n.* 生活方式	**career** *n.* 職業
spitting image *n.* 一模一樣的人或東西	**resemble** *v.* 類似
exactly *adv.* 完全地	**take after** *ph.* 相似

FAQ 中西文化外交交流的一問三答 Track 16

Q ***Why does this idiom use belt?***
為什麼這個諺語用腰帶來形容？

❶ This idiom is originally from boxing. Hitting an opponent below the belt is against the rules in boxing.

這句諺語原本是由拳擊延伸而來的。而打擊對手腰部以下為犯規的行為。

❷ It was not allowed to hit contestants below the belt in the past. It is used to condemn a politician after this idiom was invented.

在拳擊賽中，是不能打對手腰部以下的範圍。這個諺語被發明後，也用來譴責政治人物。

❸ Well, I heard it was derived from a story in boxing in the nineteenth century. Hitting below the belt was used to criticize unfair conduct.

我聽說這個是由一個在十九世紀的拳擊賽故事而來的。打擊對手腰部以下被指為一種不公平的行為。

Q Can I only relate this idiom to boxing when using it?
這個諺語只能做拳擊賽相關的應用嗎？

❶ No, it can be used in any situation as long as you want to describe someone or something is unfair.

沒有，它可以在任何情況使用，只要你想表達某人或某事為不公平。

❷ Of course not. It is usually used in business, political situations and so on.

當然不是，它通常用在商業、政治等的情況等。

❸ Many idioms were derived from ancient stories and have been used in a variety of situations nowadays.

許多諺語源自於古老的故事，但已被用在現今各式各樣的情況。

Q ***Why is the Chinese idiom* 暗箭傷人 *similar to the English idiom below the belt?***

中文諺語 暗箭傷人與英文諺語 *below the belt* 為何相似？

❶ They both denote dishonest behaviours. It's interesting to see similar idioms from different cultural backgrounds.

它們皆表示不誠實的行為。這是一個有趣的地方，源自於不同的文化背景的諺語，卻意味著相似的意思。

❷ They both are figuratively used to describe anything which is considered unscrupulous. 暗箭傷人 means attacking others by using a hidden arrow. As hitting below the belt in a boxing game, both acts are not fair and sometimes are done without others' expectation and preparation.

它們皆用來比喻形容不道德的行為。暗箭傷人意指用暗箭攻擊他人，同拳擊賽中打擊腰帶之下的行為，兩者都是不公平而且有趁人不備的意思。

❸ Well, below the belt is more colloquial but 暗箭傷人 is often used in written Chinese.

嗯，below the belt 較口語化，但暗箭傷人多用在中文的寫作上。

Vocabulary 重點單字

- **rival** *n.* 競爭對手

例：Companies launch marketing campaigns to win customers from their rivals.
企業舉辦行銷活動以從它們的競爭對手贏得客戶。

- **aggressive** *adj.* 積極進取的

例：Susan is an aggressive businesswoman and has been promoted to regional manager recently.
Susan 為一位積極進取的女商人，最近也被升為區經理。

- **unscrupulous** *adj.* 不道德的；不公正的

例：David is an unscrupulous businessman and had stolen many projects from his rivals.
David 為一位不道德的生意人，他從競爭對手中偷走許多案子。

- **foul** *n.* 比賽中的犯規行為

例：He committed a foul in a game and lost the opportunity to play in the next game.
他在比賽中犯規，並失去了下一場比賽的資格。

- **condemn** *v.* 譴責

例：The government condemned his illegal behaviour and arrested him.
政府譴責他的非法行為，並且逮捕他。

- **opponent** *n.* 敵手

例：Richard is a major opponent in the election.
Richard 為這次選舉中的主要敵手。

文化巧巧說：諺語與外交相關的文化趣事

Below the belt was originally used to denote an unfair action in boxing in the nineteenth century. However, it has been widely used in business, political situations, especially in competitions. An old Chinese idiom - 暗箭傷人 also indicates attacking your opponents sneakily and unfairly. 暗箭傷人 has been used in many old Chinese novels describing attacking enemies unscrupulously in war.

Apart from 暗箭傷人, 使技倆, 手段, 花招 (using tricks in English) are also ways to describe this situation.使技倆、手段、花招 are more colloquial and commonly used in a variety of situations in Chinese. This is an interesting point you could bring up in your conversation.

Below the belt 源自於十九世紀，用在表示拳擊賽中不公平的行為。然而，它已在商場及政治情況中廣泛地使用，特別是在指競爭的情況。中文成語－暗箭傷人也是在形容暗地裡不公平地攻擊你的對手。暗箭傷人也被許多古老的中文故事引用來形容在戰場上不道德地攻擊敵軍。

除了暗箭傷人外， 也可用使技倆、手段、花招（英文裡面的 tricks 之意）等來形容。使技倆、手段、花招為較口語化，且常被使用在各式各樣的場合。這是在會話中可提及的有趣的地方。

Unit 9 Climb/ Jump on the bandwagon 順應潮流

How to use this idiom and on what occasions you can use this idiom 這句諺語你會怎麼說、能派上用場的場合

Track 17

A bandwagon was used to attract the public's attention during a parade in the past. To climb on the bandwagon implies that you want to join a movement which is likely to become successful. When someone wants to give support or join a leading political party, you can also use this idiom to describe this situation. In addition, it is also widely used in business situations. For example, ***many companies are jumping on the bandwagon to launch their online business.***

Bandwagon在過去為遊行中用來吸引大眾的注意的樂隊車。爬上樂隊車意指加入較可能成功的行動。當某人想要支持或加入某個政黨，你可以用這個諺語來形容這個情形。除此之外，它也廣泛地被使用在商業情形。比如說，***許多公司們也順應潮流加入網路商店的行列。***

Synonyms and Analysis 中西諺語應用與翻譯

The original idiom 原來怎麼說

Climb / Jump on the bandwagon

Synonyms 還能怎麼翻

Follow the crowd, follow the trends, follow the example of, bandwagon effect

Explanations 中西諺語翻譯說明

The other word to describe this idiom is to follow the crowd. For instance, ***most companies followed the crowd to design products consumers like. Some artists wouldn't compromise with the latest trend. They refuse to change their designs in order to follow the crowd.***

The bandwagon effect is another way to describe this situation. It means people don't have their own ideas and just do something because other people are doing it.

Some Chinese idioms have similar meanings to climbing on the bandwagon, such as 隨波逐流 which originally means an object is following the wave on the ocean. It denotes people who follow the trends.

其他形容法，像是 Follow the crowd。舉例來說，***大部分的公司們皆順應潮流來設計消費者所喜愛的商品。一些藝術家們不願順應潮流，而妥協改變原設計的初衷。***

羊群效應也是一個形容這個情形的說法。它指人們沒有主見，而是人云亦云地盲從跟隨別人的做法。

一些中文慣用語也與 climb on the bandwagon 的意思相近。隨波逐流原指一個物體跟隨著海浪飄流。它暗指著人們跟著趨勢。

Analysis 中西諺語翻譯分析

Climb on the bandwagon, follow the crowd, follow the trends and follow the example of something are used as single phrases in sentences. Examples can go like this: ***Online shopping has become very popular recently; many companies tried to climb on the bandwagon.***

Climb on the bandwagon, follow the crowd, follow the trends 及follow the example of皆為用在句子中的片語。它們的應用為：***近來網路購物十分熱門，許多公司試著跟上潮流***。

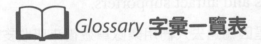

Glossary 字彙一覽表

climb *v.* 攀登	**follow the crowd** *ph.* 隨波逐流
a bandwagon effect *n.* 羊群效應	**design** *n.* 設計
refuse *v.* 拒絕	**object** *n.* 物體
wave *n.* 波浪	**online shopping** *n.* 網路購物

 FAQ 中西文化外交交流的一問三答 Track 18

Q ***Why is this idiom relevant to a bandwagon?***

為什麼這句諺語跟樂隊車相關？

❶ Parades with bandwagons were used in promoting election campaigns in the olden days. To jump on the bandwagon usually means supporting a popular political party.

樂隊車為過去用在選舉造勢的遊行中。跳上樂隊車通常指支持某一個政黨。

❷ This is relevant to American culture. People used bandwagons to parade through the streets and attract supporters.

這個跟美國的文化相關。這是因為過去人們用樂隊車遊街來吸收支持者。

❸ As you can see from this idiom, bandwagons make noises on the street and can attract the public's interest. Therefore, bandwagons were used by politicians to attract an increasing number of supporters in the past.

如原諺語所示，樂隊車在街上製造噪音及吸引大眾的目光。因此，樂隊車曾經被政治家使用來吸引更多的支持民眾。

Q **Apart from a political campaign, in what kind of situations can you use this idiom?**
除了政治造勢活動外，什麼樣的情況可使用這句諺語？

❶ You can use this idiom to describe popular trends people or companies usually follow.

你可以用來形容一些人們或公司所追求的流行的趨勢。

❷ I often hear people say “Don’t climb on the bandwagon. Have you own opinions.”

我常聽別人說：「別人云亦云，要有自己的主見。」。

❸ It can be used in business situations. Companies usually jump on the bandwagon when they see successful stories from other competitors.

這個可以用在商場上。公司們通常從競爭對手那邊看到一些成功的故事，就想追隨他們的腳步。

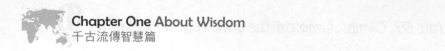

Q Can you give me more examples about using this idiom nowadays?

你可以舉更多關於這個諺語放在現代使用的例子嗎？

❶ Here is an example. Most people who queue up to buy the latest smart phones are just jumping on the bandwagon even though they have already had smart phones.

這是一個例子。即使大部分的人已經有了智慧型手機，但還是排隊購買最新出的智慧型手機，這只是在追求流行。

❷ Um. When I was a teenager, miniskirts were fashionable. Girls shortened the length of skirts to jump on the bandwagon.

嗯，當我還是一名青少年時，迷你裙很流行。女孩們皆將裙子的長度縮短以追求時尚。

❸ Well, let me show you an example. The launch of tablet PCs went successfully. Most computer manufacturers tried to jump on the bandwagon and created more tablet PCs with touch screen features.

讓我舉一個例子。平板電腦的推出十分的成功，大部分的電腦製造商也試著順應潮流來推出更多具備觸碰式螢幕功能的平板電腦。

Vocabulary 重點單字

- **movement** *n.* 行動；動向；變遷

例：There is a movement towards green architecture in the market.
市場上正吹著一股綠建築的動向。

- **compromise** *n./ v.* 妥協

例：We really hope we can reach a compromise and close the deal.
我們真的希望能妥協並完成交易。

- **election** *n.* 選舉

例：Many candidates launched aggressive campaigns in order to win the election.
大部分的參選人推出浩大的競選活動，希望贏得這場選舉。

- **parade** *n./ v.* 遊行

例：A parade will be held on Chinese New Year.
中國新年將舉行遊行。

- **tablet PCs** *n.* 平板電腦

例：Youngsters can get to know how to use Tablet PCs easily but the elderly still need time to work it out.
年輕人可輕易學會如何使用平板電腦，但老年人還需時間了解如何使用。

- **consumer behaviour** 顧客行為

例：You should observe consumer behaviour before you create any products in the market.
在開發任何產品前，你應先觀察市場顧客行為。

- **feature** *n.* 特色

例：The key feature of this holiday resort is its white sandy beach.
這個渡假地的特色為白色的沙灘。

文化巧巧說：諺語與外交相關的文化趣事

This idiom was originally derived from the movement of people who joined the bandwagon. It describes people who follow the trends and don't have their own opinions. Both English idioms - jump on the bandwagon and the Chinese idiom - 隨波逐流 indicate the same situation. They often describe people or companies following the trends or successful experiences in the political and business situations.

For a political situation, it often refers to voters who support a leading political party. For a business situation, it usually refers to companies which follow the examples of rivals' successful products or stories. It is also commonly seen in the consumer behaviour. For example, ***when people have no ideas and have to choose one restaurant from many new restaurants, they usually jump on the bandwagon and choose the most popular one.***

這句諺語原本是由人們追逐樂隊車的動向而來的。它形容人們順應潮流，沒有自己想法的情形。英文諺語 – Jump on the bandwagon 及中文諺語 – 隨波逐流皆有著相同的意思。它們通常表示群眾及公司們在政治及商業的立場上，追求成功的趨勢。

在政治情況上，它通常指有投票權的人支持領先的黨派。就商業情況來看，它通常指公司們效法競爭者成功的商品或其經歷。這在一般的顧客行為中也很常見。比如說，當人們打不定主意，不知要選哪一間新餐廳時，他們通常隨波逐流，選擇最受歡迎的一間。

Unit 10 When in Rome, do as the Romans do 入境隨俗

How to use this idiom and on what occasions you can use this idiom 這句諺語你會怎麼說、能派上用場的場合

Track 19

"When in Rome, do as the Romans do" denotes to follow the local customs when you are a visitor in a new environment or a different country. It is used as a suggestion that a new comer should adopt the local culture and behave properly. This proverb derives from a letter from St Augustine in circa 390AD. When the empire of Rome was expanding and incorporating many new citizens, the proverb then had been shortened to "When in Rome".

When in Rome, do as the Romans do 表示當你到了一個新的環境或異國時，應遵循當地的習俗。它是用來建議新到異鄉者應接受當地的文化，並遵守行為。這句諺語源自於聖奧古斯丁（St Augustine）大約在西元390年時的一封信。當羅馬帝國擴張，並接收更多的人民時，這句便縮短為 When in Rome。

Synonyms and Analysis 中西諺語應用與翻譯

The original idiom 原來怎麼說

When in Rome, do as the Romans do

Synonyms 還能怎麼翻

When in Rome, go native, blend in with something, follow the local customs, do as the local people do, adopt the local culture

Explanations 中西諺語翻譯說明

There are many other ways to describe this proverb, such as go native and blend in with something. If someone goes native, it means that he has begun to live like local people. Go native usually describe immigrants who have started to behave like local people. If you blend in with something, it means that you try to make yourself indistinguishable with the surrounding people or things.

有許多的方式可形容這句諺語，像是 Go native 或 blend in with something。假如某人 go native，表示他開始生活地像當地人。Go native 通常形容移民漸漸地表現地像當地人一樣。假如你 blend in with something，這是指你試著融入周遭，並做出與四周人相同的事。

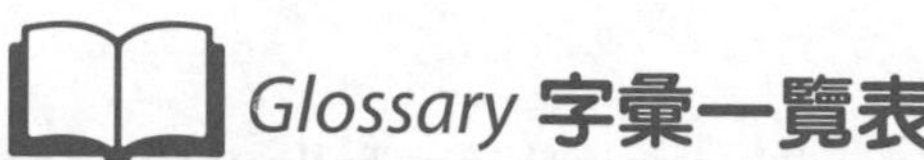

Glossary 字彙一覽表

Rome *n.* 羅馬	**Roman** *n.* 羅馬人
go native *ph.* 適應當地的生活	**blend in** *ph.* 融入
adopt *v.* 接受	**proverb** *n.* 諺語
local people *n.* 當地人	

Analysis 中西諺語翻譯分析

For go native, go is used as a verb in sentences. An example can go like this: ***Simon has lived in Japan for twenty years. He's gone native.***

Blend in with something is used as a phrasal verb in sentences. An example can go like this: ***Tom has joined a new company and tried to blend in with the new environment.***

對於 Go native 的 go 在句子中作為動詞使用。它的應用為：***Simon 在日本住了二十年，他已經像當地人一樣了***。

Blend in with something 於句子中作為片語動詞使用。***Tom 剛剛加入了一個新公司，並試著融入新環境***。

Notes

FAQ 中西文化外交交流的一問三答 Track 20

Q *How do you describe this proverb in Chinese?*
該如何用中文形容這句諺語呢？

❶ You can say 入境隨俗 or 入鄉隨俗. It means to behave like local people when you go to a new place. They are commonly used in daily conversation.

你可以說入境隨俗、或者是入鄉隨俗。它代表當一個人到了一個新的環境，表現得像當地人一樣。這句在日常會話中很常使用。

❷ Well, 隨遇而安 is another way to describe "When in Rome, do as the Romans do". It means someone can easily settle down when they move to a new environment.

隨遇而安為另一個形容 When in Rome, do as the Romans do 的方法。它表示某人很容易在新的環境中安定下來。

❸ Um, I know a Chinese idiom called 入國問俗. It means to ask the local people about their customs when you enter a new country.

嗯，我知道一句中文成語-入國問俗。它指人當到了一個新的國家時，向當地人請教他們的風俗習慣。

Q **Can you say "When in Rome, do as the Romans do" in a simple way?**
是否可用簡單的方式來形容 When in Rome, do as the Romans do 呢？

❶ Yes, you can. You can say "Do as the local people do" or "Do as the locals do".

是的，可以的。你可以用 Do as the local people do 或 Do as the locals do 來形容。

❷ Well, you can say "Follow the local customs" or "Observe the local customs".

你可以說跟隨當地習俗（Follow the local customs）或者是 觀察當地習俗（Observe the local customs）。

❸ A simple way to describe this idiom is "to adopt the local culture when you move to a new country".

簡單來說就是當你移居國外時，接受當地的文化。

Q ***I often hear people say "blend in". How do you use it in a conversation?***

我常常聽到別人說*Blend in*，請問這如何在會話中應用？

❶ To blend in can also mean mix well with something. For example, the new logo color doesn't blend in with the company's corporate identity.

Blend in 也可以表示與某物搭配佳。比如說，新的 logo 顏色和公司的企業識別不相配。

❷ To blend in usually means trying to be a part of a whole by behaving the same way.

Blend in 通常指與大多數表現一樣的行為。

❸ To blend in can be used in cooking. For example, the flour blends into the water very well.

Blend in 也可以用在烹調。舉例來說，麵粉與水混合佳。

Vocabulary 重點單字

- **custom** *n.* 習俗

  例：It is the custom to give children red envelopes on Chinese New Year's Eve.
  給小孩子紅包為中國除夕的習俗。

- **native** *n.* 本地人

  例：If you get lost in a new place, it is better to ask a native for directions.
  假如你在一個新的地方迷路，最好向本地人問路。

- **immigrant** *n.* 移民

  例：England has a large population of immigrants.
  英國有很多的移民人口。

- **surrounding** *adj.* 附近的

  例：Many people live in the surrounding area and commute to London.
  許多人住在倫敦附近，並通勤上班。

- **environment** *n.* 環境

  例：Water pollution has affected our environment significantly.
  水質污染已經嚴重地影響我們的環境。

- **settle down** *ph.* 安頓下來

  例：Polly and Gary have recently settled down and bought a house.
  Polly 和 Gary 已經安頓下來並買了一間房子。

- **corporate identity** *n.* 企業識別

  例：Corporate identity is important for a large organisation because it helps consumers to recognize its business.
  企業識別對大型企業很重要，因為它可以幫助客戶辨別其企業。

文化巧巧說：諺語與外交相關的文化趣事

When in Rome, do as the Romans do is a well-known proverb and it is in everyday use. Travelling is so convenient nowadays. When people travel to a new country, their friends and family usually advise them to follow the local customs and don't insist on remaining doing what you do in their own country.

For example, English guests give a gift to the bride and groom when they attend a wedding, but Chinese guests give a red envelope to them when they attend a wedding. When in Rome, do as the Romans do is a good expression for this situation. It suggests people to adopt the local culture when they go to a different country.

This proverb is similar to Chinese idioms -入境隨俗, 隨遇而安 and 入國問俗. It is interesting that both ancient Chinese and English advise the same thing for travellers. Understanding the local customs and culture before you go travelling can help avoid any inconvenience and misunderstanding.

When in Rome, do as the Romans do 為一個知名的諺語，並且十分地實用。現今的社會旅行愈來愈便利了。當人們到一個新的國家旅行，他們的朋友及家人通常會建議他們遵守當地的習慣，並且不要堅持維持在原國家的一些做法。

舉例來説，當英國人參加婚禮時，通常會給新郎新娘禮物。但中國人參加婚禮時，會給他們紅包。When in Rome, do as the Romans do 在這裡就是一個很好的表達方式。它建議人們到不同國家時，應接受當地的文化。

這句諺語與中文的入境隨俗、隨遇而安或入國問俗不謀而同。有趣的是，古代中文和英文皆給旅行者相同的建議。在赴國外旅行前，了解當地的文化及習俗，可避免一些不便及誤會。

拼勁勇氣篇

About Courage

中文裡有許多用來鼓勵人們行善的慣用語。「種瓜得瓜，種豆得豆」就是一個很好的例子。這也與英文的*As you sow, so shall you reap*不謀而合。*As you sow, so shall you reap*源自於聖經，主要目的為鼓勵人們做善事，得善報。

Unit 01 *As you sow, so shall you reap*
種豆得豆，種瓜得瓜

Unit 02 *Burn the midnight oil*
挑燈夜戰

Unit 03 *Faith will move mountains*
精誠所至，金石為開

Unit 04 *Bend over backwards*
全力以赴

Unit 05 *Face the music*
面對現實

Unit 06 *Take the bull by the horns*
兵來將擋，水來土掩

Unit 1 As you sow, so shall you reap 種瓜得瓜，種豆得豆

How to use this idiom and on what occasions you can use this idiom
這句諺語你會怎麼說、能派上用場的場合

Track 21

As you sow, so shall you reap is originally from the Bible and means how much you get depends on how hard you work. The purpose of this idiom is to encourage people to behave well to get a good result. Interestingly, there are many similar idioms in Chinese to describe this situation. For examples, 種瓜得瓜，種豆得豆 and 一分耕耘，一分收穫.

As you sow, so shall you reap 源自於聖經，它指收穫多少來自於付出多少。這句諺語的主要目的為鼓勵人們做善事，得善報。有趣的是，中文裡也有許多類似的成語，像是種瓜得瓜，種豆得豆、一分耕耘，一分收穫、善有善報，惡有惡報等等。

Synonyms and Analysis 中西諺語應用與翻譯

The original idiom 原來怎麼說

As you sow, so shall you reap

Synonyms 還能怎麼翻

As a man sows, so shall he reap; there's no such thing as a free lunch; no pain, no gain

Explanations 中西諺語翻譯說明

Apart from "As you sow, so shall you reap", you can also say "As a man sows, so shall he reap" and "As ye sow, so shall ye reap". Another way to describe this idiom is "There's no such thing as a free lunch". Literally speaking, it means that you can't get free things by doing nothing. It is used to encourage people to work hard to get what they want. This idiom delivers the same idea as "As you sow, so shall you reap".

The Chinese version of "as you sow, so shall you reap"- 種瓜得瓜，種豆得豆 describes that you get melons if you sow melons and you get beans if you sow beans. It denotes the same idea as "As a man sows, so shall he reap" to encourage people to do good things in order to get rewards.

No pain, no gain is another similar way to describe “As you sow, so shall you reap”. It means that you have to work hard in order to make progress. However, no pain no gain is often used in sports or physical training. For example, ***Athlete: I can’t do it anymore. Coach: You have to work hard to win gold medals in the Olympics. No pain, no gain.***

除了 As you sow, so shall you reap 外，它也可以稱為 As a man sows, so shall he reap。另一個形容法為天下沒有白吃的午餐（There’s no such thing as a free lunch.）。字面上來看，它指的是無法不做任何事，而取得免費的東西。它是用來鼓勵人們辛勤工作，以獲得所需的物品。這句諺語與 As you sow, so shall you reap 傳達著相同的理念。

中文版的 As you sow, so shall you reap 為種瓜得瓜，種豆得豆。它表示種什麼因，得什麼果的意思。它與 As you sow, so shall you reap 皆在勸導人們做善事，得善報。

No pain, no gain 為另一個形容 “As you sow, so shall you reap” 的相似詞。它指你必需努力，才能進步。然而，No pain, no gain 通常用在運動及體能訓練上。舉例來說：*運動員：我沒辦法再繼續下去了。教練：你必需努力，才能在奧運拿下金牌。沒有辛勞，哪來收穫。*

Analysis 中西諺語翻譯分析

"As you sow, so shall you reap" and "There's no such thing as a free lunch" are used as single phrases in sentences. For example, ***Johnny always treats people nicely. As you sow, so shall you reap. He is so popular and has many friends. There's no such thing as a free lunch, you need to be realistic.***

As you sow, so shall you reap 及 There's no such thing as a free lunch 皆在句子中做為單一片語使用。舉例來說，***Johnny 總是善待他人。種瓜得瓜，種豆得豆，他現在很受歡迎，且廣結善緣。天下沒有白吃的午餐，實際點吧。***

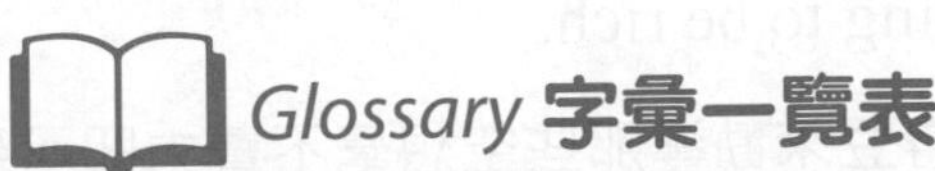

Glossary 字彙一覽表

sow *v.* 播種	**There's no such thing as a free lunch.** 天下沒有白吃的午餐
deliver *v.* 傳達	**encourage** *v.* 鼓勵
progress *n.* 進步	**coach** *n.* 教練
gold medal *n.* 金牌	**Olympics** *n.* 奧林匹克

FAQ 中西文化外交交流的一問三答 Track 22

Q ***Are there any idioms similar to "As you sow, so shall you reap" in Chinese?***

在中文中，有哪些諺語與 ***As you sow, so shall you reap*** 相同？

❶ Yes, a similar idiom is 一分耕耘，一分收穫. It means what you reap is what you sow.

是的，它相似的成語為一分耕耘，一分收穫。它指的是怎麼收穫，怎麼栽的意思。

❷ Well, I usually use 種瓜得瓜，種豆得豆 to encourage my friends who believe they can do nothing to be rich.

嗯，我通常用種瓜得瓜，種豆得豆來勸導那些空想毫不費力即可致富的朋友們。

❸ There are many ways to describe this idiom. 天下沒有白吃的午餐 is a good example. It means nothing is free in the world.

有很多方法可以形容這句諺語。像是天下沒有白吃的午餐就是一個很好的例子。它指的是世界上沒有不勞而獲的事物。

Q What are the differences between "as you sow, so shall you reap" and "no pain, no gain"?
那麼 so shall you reap 及 no pain, no gain 有什麼不同？

❶ As you sow, so shall you reap usually indicates how you behave will affect how other people treat you. "No pain, no gain" encourages people to work harder to get good results.

As you sow, so shall you reap 通常指的是你的待人處世會影響別人怎麼對待你。而 No pain, no gain 為鼓勵人們努力工作，以獲得好的成果。

❷ Well, they are similar. Both "as you sow, so shall you reap" and "no pain, no gain" are used to persuade people to work harder or behave well to get rewards.

A: 嗯，它們非常的相似。 As you sow, so shall you reap 及 No pain, no gain 的用意皆在說服人們努力工作、或善待他人，以獲得好的回報。

❸ "No pain, no gain" is usually used in sports training.

No pain, no gain 通常是用在運動訓練上。

Q Can you please give me more examples of these idioms?
你可以舉更多關於這些諺語的例子嗎？

❶ When my colleagues found out Maggie is a backstabber, they stopped talking to her. As you sow, so shall you reap.

當我的同事發現 Maggie 為在背後說人壞話的人後，即停止跟她說話。種瓜得瓜，種豆得豆。

❷ Here is an example. A salesman said they can give me a free TV if I register with them. I think there's no such thing as a free lunch.

這裡有個例子。一個銷售人員說假如我跟他們註冊的話，他們可以免費給我一台電視。我認為天下沒有白吃的午餐。

❸ I don't like doing exercise but I am overweight. I need to lose weight. No pain, no gain.

我討厭運動，但是我過重了。我必需減重，沒有辛勞，哪來收穫。

Vocabulary 重點單字

- **reap** *v.* 收割

例：Farmers have been busy all year and waited for reaping the rice from the farm. 農夫們辛苦一年，並等著在田裡收割稻米。

- **reward** *n.* 報償

例：Jenny has been working so hard in the past decade. Her company gave her a gift as a reward for her hard work.
Jenny 在過去的十年中辛苦工作。她的公司送給她一個禮品做為她辛勤工作的回報。

- **realistic** *adj.* 實際的

例：Competition is fierce. You need to be realistic to run a business. 競爭很激烈。你做生意必需務實。

- **backstabber** *n.* 背後說人壞話者

例：A backstabber usually ends up in a difficult situation as people will find out what they have done eventually.
背後說人壞話者通常的結局皆不好，因為人們最後會發現他們的所作所為。

- **overweight** *adj.* 超重的

例：She used to be overweight. A healthy diet made her lose weight.她曾經過重。健康的飲食幫助她減重。

- **physical training** *n.* 體能訓練

例：Jeff is a professional athlete. He had been receiving physical training since he was a teenager.
Jeff 為專業的運動員。他自青少年以來就開始接受體能訓練。

- **athlete** *n.* 運動員

例：The life of athletes is healthy. They do regular exercise and have a strict diet.
運動員的生活很健康。他們規律地運動，並有著嚴格的飲食計劃。

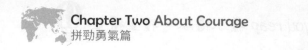

文化巧巧說：諺語與外交相關的文化趣事

As you sow, so shall you reap derives from the Bible and is used in a situation when you try to encourage people to behave well for a better life. Apart from this idiom, many similar phrases have been developed over time, such as "There's no such thing as a free lunch", and "No pain, no gain".

The similar Chinese idioms include 種瓜得瓜，種豆得豆，一分耕耘，一分收穫，善有善報，惡有惡報 and 天下沒有白吃的午餐. They derived from the ancient China and are commonly used in daily conversation. You can bring up the similarity between the Chinese and English idioms when you talk to your friends or clients.

As you sow, so shall you reap 源自於聖經，並且用在鼓勵人們做好事、得好報。除了這句諺語外，許多相似的慣用語也隨時間不斷發展，像是 There's no such thing as a free lunch 及 No pain, no gain。

中文的諺語包括種瓜得瓜，種豆得豆、一分耕耘，一分收穫、善有善報，惡有惡報。這些都是千古流傳的名言，並實用於日常生活中。當你與朋友及客户聊天時，你可以提及這個中西文化上共通點。

Unit 2 Burn the midnight oil 挑燈夜戰

How to use this idiom and on what occasions you can use this idiom
這句諺語你會怎麼說、能派上用場的場合

Track 23

Before the invention of electricity, people used oil lamps or candles at night. As you can see from the original idiom, it means to work very late past midnight. 挑燈夜戰 is a relevant Chinese idiom. It means working late past midnight in order to finish something. It was usually used when someone was preparing exams in the past.

在電力發明前，人們在夜晚使用油燈或蠟燭。從字面上來看，它指工作到半夜。挑燈夜戰為相關的中文成語。它指工作到深夜，以完成某事。它在過去通常用在準備考試。

Synonyms and Analysis 中西諺語應用與翻譯

The original idiom 原來怎麼說

Burn the midnight oil

Synonyms 還能怎麼翻

Work overtime, stay up, bear down, work hard, work late, work like a dog

Explanations 中西諺語翻譯說明

"Bear down" has the similar meaning as "Burn the midnight oil". Its example can go like this: ***I have to bear down to complete this project as its deadline is coming.*** "Work overtime", "stay up" and "work late" indicate extra hours you spend to finish something. For instance, ***since we have received many orders recently, I have to work overtime to finish all the deliveries. Susan stayed up all night studying.***

"Work like a dog" is another way to indicate working very hard. It is using the word "dog" in a figurative sense.

Bear down 也與 Burn the midnight oil 有著相似的意思。它的例子為：***交期在即，我必需專心致力於完成這個案子***。Work overtime、stay up 及 work late 指需額外花時間來完成某事。比如說，***由於最近收到很多訂單，我必需加班工作來完成出貨。Susan 一晚不睡來學習。***

Work like a dog 也是用來形容努力工作的一個慣用語。這是用狗（dog）做為比喻的方式。

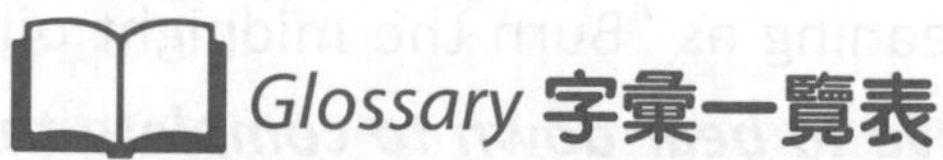

Glossary 字彙一覽表

work like a dog *ph.* 拼命地工作	**deadline** *n.* 交期
delivery *n.* 交貨	**work overtime** *ph.* 超時工作
extra hours *n.* 超出的工時	**business owner** *n.* 企業經營者
profit *n.* 利潤	**midnight** *n.* 午夜

Analysis 中西諺語翻譯分析

"Burn the midnight oil" and "work like a dog" are used as single phrases in sentences. For instance, ***students usually burn the midnight oil before exams. Burn the midnight oil is not good for your health. You should go to bed early. Business owners worked like a dog all day to make more profits for their companies.***

"Stay up" and "bear down" are used as phrasal verbs in sentences. Examples can go like this: ***Alan stayed up to play computer games. You have failed an exam last time, you have to bear down and pass the test.***

Burn the midnight oil 及 Work like a dog 皆在句子中作為單一片語使用。例如，***學生通常挑燈夜戰來準備考試。挑燈夜戰對你的健康不好。你應該早點上床睡覺。生意人努力工作，為他們的公司賺取更多的利潤。***

Stay up 及 Bear down 為在句子中作為片語動詞。它們的應用為：***Alan 一整晚不睡來玩電腦遊戲。你上次考試不及格，你必需更努力來通過考試。***

FAQ 中西文化外交交流的一問三答 Track 24

Q ***What is the origin of "burning the midnight oil?"***
***Burn the midnight oil* 的起源為？**

❶ The similar expression was mentioned in the seventeenth century. This idiom is still in everyday use even though people don't use oil lamps anymore.

它的相似詞在十七世紀時被提及。即使人們不再用油燈，這個諺語還是被人們廣泛地使用。

❷ Well, the literal meaning of "burning the midnight oil" is lighting a candle or oil lamp at night. It denotes working very late.

嗯，從字面上來看，這是指半夜燒蠟燭及油燈。引伸為工作到很晚。

❸ Before we created electricity, people used candlelight working at night. So this phrase is used figuratively and means staying up very late.

在我們發明電力前，古代人在半夜點蠟燭工作。所以這個諺語為比喻工作到很晚。

Q What are the relevant idioms in Chinese?
其他相關的中文諺語為？

❶ There are many ways to describe "burning the midnight oil" in Chinese, such as 三更燈火五更雞, 熬夜 and 開夜車.

中文裡有很多方法來表示 Burn the midnight oil，像是三更燈火五更雞、熬夜及開夜車。

❷ 挑燈夜戰 is very similar to "buring the midnight oil" because both describe staying up at night by using oil lamps.

挑燈夜戰非常接近 Burn the midnight oil，因為它們皆使用油燈來表達工作到很晚。

❸ You can say 開夜車 in Chinese, meaning driving at night. Compared with 挑燈夜戰, 開夜車 is more colloquial.

你還可以說開夜車，也就是晚上開車的意思。與挑燈夜戰相比，開夜車較口語化。

Q When can you use "burn the midnight oil"?
在什麼樣的情況可使用 *Burn the midnight oil*？

❶ This idiom is often used when someone needs to study and work at night.

這句諺語通常用形容必須在晚上學習及工作。

❷ Let me show you an example. I have got a lot of work to do recently. I even have to burn the midnight oil at home.

讓我舉一個例子。我最近的工作量大增，我甚至還要回家熬夜加班。

❸ Well, it's commonly used in daily conversation. For instance, students usually burn the midnight oil to prepare exams.

嗯，它很常用在日常對話中。如，學生們通常熬夜準備考試。

Vocabulary 重點單字

- **invention** *n.* 發明

例：Mobile phone is a great invention. Many people benefit from this device.
手機為一個偉大的發明。許多人皆受益於使用它。

- **oil lamp** *n.* 油燈

例：People used oil lamps to read at night in the past.
古代人在晚上使用油燈。

- **stay up** *v.* 不睡覺

例：I stay up because my project's deadline is tomorrow. I worry that I can't finish it.
因為交期在明天，我擔心無法完成，而熬夜加班。

- **phrasal verb** *n.* 動詞片語

例：Watch out and look after are phrasal verbs.
Watch out 及 look after 皆為動詞片語。

- **literal** *adj.* 照字面的

例：The literal meaning of this word is very easy to understand.
這個字的字面意義十分容易理解。

- **a variety of** *ph.* 各式各樣的

例：Taiwan has perfect weather to plant a variety of fruit and vegetables.
台灣的天氣適合種植各式各樣的水果及蔬菜。

- **figurative** *adj.* 比喻的

例：This idiom is used in a figurative sense.
這個諺語為用來比喻。

文化巧巧說：諺語與外交相關的文化趣事

The relevant sentences about working late had been recorded in the seventeenth century. Both ancient Chinese and English have the similar phrases to express working into the midnight. Interestingly, both burn the midnight oil and 挑燈夜戰 are using an oil lamp as an example. The similarity between "Burn the midnight oil" and "挑燈夜戰" can help you to memorize these phrases and use them in conversation.

Apart from 挑燈夜戰, there are many Chinese idioms describing working into the midnight, such as 三更燈火五更雞, 開夜車 and 熬夜. The literal meaning of 三更燈火五更雞 is going to bed late but waking up early. It denotes working very hard. Both 開夜車 and 熬夜 are colloquial and means staying up.

與熬夜工作相關的詞句曾在十七世紀時所記載。中文及英文皆有許多相近的慣用語來表達工作到半夜。有趣的是，Burn the midnight oil 及挑燈夜戰皆用油燈做為例子。Burn the midnight oil 及挑燈夜戰的相似之處可幫助你記憶此慣用語，並活用於日常會話中。

除了挑燈夜戰外，其他形容工作到半夜的慣用語還有三更燈火五更雞、開夜車、熬夜。三更燈火五更雞為形容晚睡早起，它意指辛勞工作。開夜車及熬夜為口語化表達不睡覺的意思。

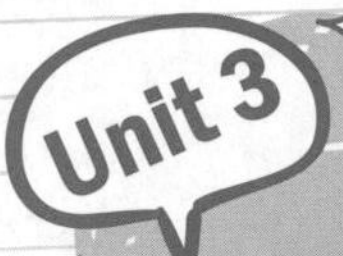

Unit 3 Faith will move mountains 精誠所至，金石為開

How to use this idiom and on what occasions you can use this idiom 這句諺語你會怎麼說、能派上用場的場合

Track 25

This proverb was originally from the Bible. It denotes you can achieve something if you believe you can do it. People usually use this proverb to encourage people when they encounter difficulties in their lives. For example, ***you might think it's impossible to complete this task but faith will move mountains.*** This is similar to Chinese phrases - 精誠所至，金石為開, 有志者事竟成 or 鐵杵磨成針.

這句諺語原本來自於聖經。它象徵著只要你相信自己能做得到，就能達成某件事。一般人通常用這句諺語來鼓勵那些在生命中遭遇困難的人。舉例來說，***你也許認為不可能會完成這個任務，但是有志者事竟成***。這也與中文的精誠所至，金石為開、有志者事竟成及鐵杵磨成針等有著異曲同工之妙。

Synonyms and Analysis 中西諺語應用與翻譯

The original idiom 原來怎麼說

Faith will move mountains

Synonyms 還能怎麼翻

Move mountains, where there's a will there's a way

Explanations 中西諺語翻譯說明

There are the other ways to describe this proverb, such as "move mountains" and "where there's a will there's a way." "Move mountains" means achieving something impossible. For example, ***if we believe that we can move mountains, we will succeed.*** Move mountains also means that do your best to please someone. For instance, ***Rita moved mountains for the company but she was dismissed unfairly.***

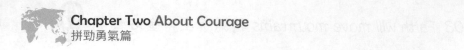

"Where there's a will there's a way" indicates that it is possible to achieve what you want if you persevere with what you are doing. For example, ***this is what I want to do. I'll work hard to achieve my goal even though it is very difficult. Where there's a will there's a way.***

其他形容 faith will move mountains 的形容法有 move mountains 及 where there's a will there's a way。Move mountains 指達成某件幾乎不可能完成的事。比如說，***假如我們認為我們辦的到，我們就會成功***。Move mountains 也表示*竭盡全力去討好某人*。舉例來說，***Rita 竭盡全力為公司付出，但卻被不公平地解僱了。***

Where there's a will there's a way 表示假如你堅持到底，即有可能會心想事成。例如，***這就是我想做的事。即使這件事很困難，但我會努力完成目標。有志者事竟成。***

Analysis 中西諺語翻譯分析

"Faith will move mountains" and "where there's a will there's a way" are usually used as single phrases in sentences. Examples can go like this: ***Don't feel frustrated. Please remember that faith will move mountains. I'm going to move overseas next month. I have no friends and family there but where there's a will there's a way.***

Faith will move mountains 及 where there's a will there's a way 通常於句中作為單一片語。舉例如下：***別感到挫敗。請記得有志者事竟成。我下個月要移居海外。我在那沒有親人朋友，但是我相信有志者事竟成。***

Glossary 字彙一覽表

Where there's a will there's a way. 有志者事竟成	**achieve** *v.* 達成
impossible *adj.* 不可能的	**dismiss** *v.* 解僱
goal *n.* 目的	**frustrated** *adj.* 挫敗的
faith *n.* 信念	**overseas** *adv.* 在海外

FAQ 中西文化外交交流的一問三答 Track 26

Q ***What are the other ways you can describe this proverb in Chinese?***

還有什麼可用中文形容此諺語的方法？

❶ Well, 有志者事竟成 is a well-known Chinese idiom describing you will achieve your goal if you are determined.

有志者事竟成為一個家喻戶曉的成語，它描述只要下定決心，就能達成目標。

❷ You can say 鐵杵磨成針. Its literal meaning is an iron pestle can be ground into a needle. It denotes you will obtain something you want if you work very hard.

你可以說鐵杵磨成針。它如同字面上的意思，只要努力，即使鐵杵也能磨成針。比喻著有努力就有收穫。

❸ The literal meaning of 天下無難事 is nothing is impossible in the world. It denotes that nothing is impossible if you are determined.

天下無難事字面上的意思為世界上沒有什麼不可能完成的事。它象徵著只要下定決心，就能完成，即使是那些不可能完成的事。

Q Can you describe "faith will move mountains" in a simple way?

Faith will move mountains 如何用簡單的方式來形容呢？

❶ You can simply say if you persevere your determination towards your goal, you will overcome all the obstacles.

簡單來說，你可以講假使你堅持到底，你就會克服所有的障礙。

❷ If you believe that you can do it, you will achieve your target eventually.

假如你相信你可以做到，你最後就能達到你的目標。

❸ Here is an example. If you are determined and believe in yourself, you will succeed no matter what difficulties you meet.

這裡有一個例子。假如你夠堅定，並相信自己。無論遇到什麼困難，你也會成功。

Q ***I heard the phrase "Move mountains" has two definitions. Can you give me some examples?***

我聽說 *Move mountains* 有兩個定義。你可以舉更多例子嗎？

❶ Well, it means "do something impossible" or "make every effort to do something."

它指做一些幾乎不可能的事。或者是竭盡全力去做某件事。

❷ If it means "do something impossible", you can say "if our team believes we can move mountains, we'll win this game".

假如指完成某些不可能的事時，你可以說如果我們相信我們能辦得到，我們就會贏得這場比賽。

❸ If it means "make every effort to do something", here is an example: This is a difficult project. We have moved mountains to complete this project on time.

假如指竭盡全力去做某件事，它的例子為：這是一個困難的任務，我們竭盡全力去準時完成它。

Vocabulary 重點單字

- **encounter** *v.* 遭遇

例：When he encounters difficulties, he always tries his best to resolve them.
當他遭遇到一些困難時，他總是盡全力去解決這些困難。

- **persevere** *v.* 堅持不懈

例：Although this project has failed many times, Tommy persevered with his work.
雖然這個任務已經失敗了好幾次，Tommy 仍堅持不懈地進行。

- **determined** *adj.* 下定決心的

例：Becky is determined to win this contract from her competitor.
Becky下定決心去從競爭者手邊贏得這個合約。

- **pestle** *n.* 杵

例：Chinese medicine often uses a pestle and a mortar to crush the herbs.
中藥通常用杵臼將藥草搗碎。

- **grind** *v.* 磨碎

例：She uses a coffee grinder to grind coffee.
她用咖啡研磨機來磨碎咖啡豆。

- **obstacle** *n.* 障礙

例：You might face many obstacles in this project. Please be prepared to overcome these obstacles.
你也許會在此次任務中面對許多障礙。請準備去克服這些障礙。

- **eventually** *adv.* 最後

例：Maggie bullied many people in the company. She was dismissed from her job eventually.
Maggie 在公司中欺負很多人。她終究被解僱。

文化巧巧說：諺語與外交相關的文化趣事

Both Chinese and English have similar phrases to encourage people to work hard and believe in themselves. There are many similar ways to express "Faith will move mountains" in Chinese, such as 精誠所至, 金石為開, 有志者事竟成, 鐵杵磨成針, 人定勝天 or 天下無難事.

Both 精誠所至，金石為開 and 鐵杵磨成針 are used in figurative senses. The literal meaning of 精誠所至，金石為開 is if you make every effort, even metal or rocks can be broken up. It is used to encourage people to believe themselves that they can achieve something impossible if they do their best.

The literal meaning of 鐵杵磨成針 is an iron pestle can be ground into a needle. According to an ancient Chinese story, a young Chinese poet saw an old lady trying to grind an iron pestle into a needle. It made him realize that he could succeed one day if he persevered with his studies. He became a well-known Chinese poet eventually. This is an interesting story that shows how Chinese phrases are developed.

中文和英文兩者皆有類似的成語來鼓勵人們努力及相信自己。中文中有許多相似的成語來描述 Faith will move mountains，像是精誠所至，金石為開、有志者事竟成、鐵杵磨成針、人定勝天或天下無難事。

像是精誠所至，金石為開、及鐵杵磨成針是以比喻的方式來描述。精誠所至，金石為開字面上的意思為假如你竭盡全力，連金屬或石頭都會為之裂開。這句成語用來鼓勵人們，若盡全力去做某事，連極不可能發生的事都能順利完成。

鐵杵磨成針就如同字面上的意思。根據一個古老的中國故事，一位年輕的詩人看見一位老太太試著將一支鐵杵磨成針。這使他領悟到只要他堅持不懈地認真讀書，有朝一日會成功的。他最後成為了一位知名的中國詩人。這個有趣的故事，也說明著中國成語的演進。

Unit 4

Bend over backwards
全力以赴

How to use this idiom and on what occasions you can use this idiom
這句諺語你會怎麼說、能派上用場的場合

Track 27

"Bend over backwards" means to strenuously do something to please someone. People usually use this phrase to express someone who makes every effort to complete something. It can also be used in a negative way to describe someone who doesn't appreciate what you have done. For example, ***Simon bent over backwards for you, but you still think it's not good enough.*** This phrase is similar to 竭盡全力 or 全力以赴 in Chinese.

Bend over backwards 指某人盡力去做某事、或討好某人。人們通常用這句慣用語來表達盡力去完成一些事。它也可以用負面的方式來形容他人並不感激你所做的努力。舉例來說，***Simon 盡全力幫你，但你還是覺得不夠好***。這句慣用語與中文的竭盡全力、或全力以赴有異曲同工之妙。

Synonyms and Analysis 中西諺語應用與翻譯

The original idiom 原來怎麼說

Bend over backwards

Synonyms 還能怎麼翻

Lean over backwards, do one's best, make every effort, go all out, break one's neck.

Explanations 中西諺語翻譯說明

There are many ways to describe this phrase, such as lean over backwards, do one's best, make every effort, go all out or break one's neck. "Make every effort" means working very hard to achieve something. "Go all out" means trying everything possible for something you want to achieve.

Break one's neck is an interesting expression. It is used in a figurative sense. It indicates to work very hard to accomplish something. For instance, ***Ruby has been breaking her neck to solve this problem for her family.***

有許多方式來描述 bend over backwards，像是 lean over backwards、do one's best、make every effort、go all out、或 break one's neck。Make every effort 指努力工作來達成某事。Go all out 則是表示盡所有可能來達成你所想要完成的事。

Break one's neck 為一個有趣的表達方式。它是在比喻的意義上使用。它意指全力以赴來達成某事。比如說，***Ruby 全力以赴為她的家人解決問題。***

Notes

Analysis 中西諺語翻譯分析

"Bend over backwards", "lean over backwards" and "go all out" are usually put after subjects in sentences. Examples can go like this: ***Alan bent over backwards to help his customers. The team went all out to make the marketing campaign a success.***

Bend over backwards、lean over backwards 及 go all out 通常於句中置於主詞之後。舉例來說，***Alan 竭盡全力幫助他的客戶。整個團隊全力以赴，以讓行銷活動大獲全勝。***

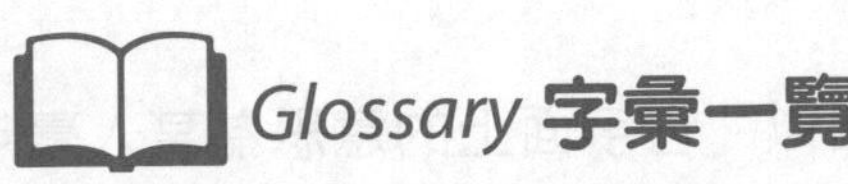

Glossary 字彙一覽表

backwards *adv.* 向後	**lean** *v.* 傾斜
go all out *ph.* 竭盡全力	**break one's neck** *ph.* 盡力做好某事
expression *n.* 詞句	**marketing** *n.* 行銷
campaign *n.* 活動	

FAQ 中西文化外交交流的一問三答 Track 28

Q How do you describe "bend over backwards" in Chinese?

請問如何用中文來敘述 Bend over backwards？

❶ You can say 全力以赴 or 盡心盡力. It indicates someone who exerts himself to do something.

你可以說全力以赴或者是盡心盡力。它指某人竭盡全力來做某事。

❷ Well, 不遺餘力 is similar to "bend over backwards". Its literal meaning is someone who has exerted all his strength and nothing has left.

不遺餘力與 Bend over backwards 相似。它字面上的意思為某人毫無保留地用盡全力。

❸ 費盡心機 is a similar phrase but has slightly different meaning. It describes someone who has thought about all the possibilities or ways to resolve something.

費盡心機為相似的用法，但稍微不同。它表示某人想盡所有的可行性或方法來解決某事。

Q What are antonyms of "bend over backwards" in Chinese?

請問 Bend over backwards 中文的反義詞為何？

❶ Well, 敷衍了事 is a good example. It describes someone who doesn't want to do something seriously and just wants to finish it quickly.

敷衍了事是一個好的例子。它形容某人因不想認真做事，而草草了事。

❷ 馬馬虎虎 is opposite to someone who wants to do a perfect job.

馬馬虎虎與一絲不苟相反。

❸ 隨隨便便 is another similar expression. It indicates someone who doesn't have an eye for detail.

隨隨便便也是一個類似的形容詞。它指某人不仔細做事。

Q What is the difference between "break one's back" and "go all out"?

請問 Break one's back 和 go all out 有何不同？

❶ Well, as you can see from the literal meaning, "break one's back" is used in a figurative sense. It means making an effort to do something. It is similar to "bend over backwards".

從字面上來看，Break one's back 是在比喻的意義上使用。它指竭盡全力去做某件事。這也與 Bend over backwards 的形容法不謀而同。

❷ "Go all out" is usually used to describe putting your enthusiasm or effort into something. It is often used for some tasks you are doing.

Go all out 通常用在形容將熱忱及精力放在某件事上。它通常用來形容某些你致力於的任務。

❸ Um, they are very similar but slightly different. "Go all out" is often used in something you are interested or something you want to achieve. For example, an event you are organizing or a match which you are playing in.

兩者皆十分類似，但有些許不同。Go all out 通常用於一些你有興趣的事物，或想達成的事上，像是你所舉辦的活動，或參加的比賽。

Vocabulary 重點單字

- **accomplish** *v.* 達到

  例：The team has accomplished their mission on time.
  這個團隊已準時達成他們的任務。

- **exert** *v.* 施加

  例：He is good at exerting his influence on other people.
  他擅於對他人施加影響力。

- **strength** *n.* 力氣

  例：Girls usually don't have enough strength to move heavy furniture.
  女孩們通常沒有太大的力氣來搬傢俱。

- **have an eye for** *ph.* 對……有鑑賞力

  例：Susan has an eye for detail. She always finds mistakes in reports.
  Susan 觀察敏銳。她總是從報告中找出錯誤來。

- **effort** *n.* 努力

  例：We should make an effort to use public transport. So we could reduce the air pollution.
  我們應該盡力使用大眾交通工具。這樣可降低空氣污染。

- **resolve** *v.* 解決

  例：This problem is difficult to be resolved and required a lot of time and money.
  這個問題很難解決，並且需要很多金錢和時間。

- **enthusiasm** *n.* 熱情

  例：After losing many games, he lost his enthusiasm for football.
  在輸了多次比賽後，他失去對足球的熱情。

文化巧巧說：諺語與外交相關的文化趣事

People usually use "do one's best" to describe working very hard in order to achieve something. Apart from "do one's best", you can also say bend over backwards to express how hard you have worked. "Break one's neck" is another similar expression. Both "bend over backwards" and "break one's neck" are used in a figurative sense and are commonly used in daily conversation, especially for showing people their efforts.

There are many ways to express work very hard in Chinese, such as 盡心盡力 or 費盡心機. As you can see from their literal meanings, they mean someone has exerted all his strength and no more to give. This idea is similar to "bend over backwards". When you talk to your clients or friends, you can also let them know the similarity between the English and Chinese phrases.

一般都是用 Do one's best 來形容努力達成某事。除了 Do one's best 以外，也可以用 bend over backwards 來表示你多麼地努力。Break one's neck 為另一個類似的表達方式。Bend over backwards 及 break one's neck 兩者皆以比喻的方式使用，並廣泛地使用於日常會話中。特別是向他人表示你的努力。

中文中有許多的形容法來表示努力工作，像是盡心盡力、或費盡心機。從字面上的意思來看，他們指某人毫無保留，用盡全力去做某事。這也與 Bend over backwards 的意義相似。當你和客戶或朋友對話時，可以讓他們了解英文與中文慣用語之間的相似之處。

Face the music
面對現實

How to use this idiom and on what occasions you can use this idiom
這句諺語你會怎麼說、能派上用場的場合

Track 29

"Face the music" means to confront unpleasant consequences for something you have done in the past. People usually say it when they know they will receive punishment for an error. For example, ***Gary has lost a contract with an important client. Now he has to go back to his company and face the music.*** This phrase is similar to 面對現實 or 承擔後果 in Chinese.

Face the music指面對及承擔自己行為的後果。人們通常在知道他們即將為錯誤而接受懲罰時，以此句來表達其心境。舉例來說，***Gary失去一個重要客戶的案子。他回到公司後，將要面對現實了***。這句慣用語也與中文的面對現實或承擔後果相似。

Synonyms and Analysis 中西諺語應用與翻譯

The original idiom 原來怎麼說

Face the music

Synonyms 還能怎麼翻

Face the facts, face up to, grin and bear it, bite the bullet, take one's lumps, face it

Explanations 中西諺語翻譯說明

There are many ways to describe face the music in English, such as face the facts, face up to, grin and bear it, bite the bullet or take one's lumps. "Grin and bear it" is an interesting expression but it is slightly different from" face the music". It indicates someone has to endure something bad without complaints. People usually say it when they have to do something they don't want to do. For example, ***I don't really like having a meeting with Maggie but I guess I'll have to grin and bear it.***

“Bite the bullet” is another similar expression. It means to face an unpleasant situation bravely. People usually say it when they have to force themselves to do something difficult. For instance, ***Simon hates needles, but he’ll have to bite the bullet.***

英語中有許多方式來形容 Face the music，像是 face the facts、face up to、grin and bear it、bite the bullet、或 take one’s lumps。Grin and bear it 為一個有趣的慣用語，但與 Face the music 些許不同。它表示某人必需忍受某些不好的事，而且不能抱怨。人們通常在必需做些不想做的事時，以此句來表達其心境。比如說，***我不想跟 Maggie 開會，但我想我必需要默默忍受。***

Bite the bullet 為另一個形容法。它指勇敢面對一些不愉快的情況。此句通常用於當要硬著頭皮去面對一些困難的情況。舉例來說，***Simon 討厭打針，但他要咬緊牙關去面對。***

Notes

Analysis 中西諺語翻譯分析

Face the facts, face up to, grin and bear it, bite the bullet and take one's lumps are usually used as single phrases in sentences. An example can go like this: ***David and Jane have to face up to the possibility of losing their house.***

Face the facts、face up to、grin and bear it、bite the bullet、及 take one's lumps 通常置於句中作為單一片語使用。舉例來說：***David 和 Jane 必需勇敢面對失去房子的可能性。***

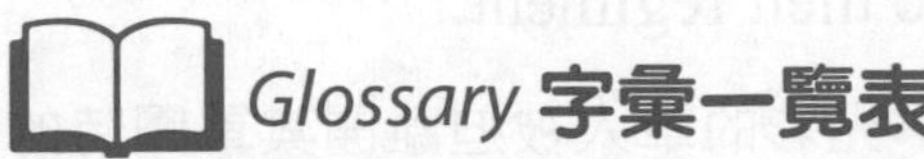

face up to *ph.* 勇於面對	**bullet** *n.* 子彈
grin and bear it *ph.* 默默忍受	**slightly** *adv.* 稍微地
endure *v.* 忍受	**unpleasant** *adj.* 令人不愉快的
bravely *adv.* 勇敢地	

FAQ 中西文化外交交流的一問三答 Track 30

Q ***What is the origin of "face the music"?***
Face the music的起源為？

❶ Its origin has been lost but some people suggest that it might be referring to actors who have to face an orchestra pit.

它的起源已遺失，但一些人建議它的起源應與演員需勇敢面對樂池來表演有關。

❷ Some people suggest that it's derived from disgraceful officers who have been forced to leave their regiment.

有些人建議它的起源應為一些不光彩的軍人被迫離開其軍團時的情形。

❸ Well, the origin of this phrase was unclear but it appeared in a newspaper in the middle of the nineteenth century.

它的起源不是很明確，但它曾於十九世紀中時出現在報紙裡。

Q How do you describe "face the music" in Chinese?
請問如何用中文形容 *Face the music*？

❶ You can simply say 勇敢地面對現實. Its literal meaning is to face the reality in a brave way.

簡單來說，可以用勇敢地面對現實來形容。

❷ 承擔後果 is another way to describe it in Chinese. It means to accept the consequences of your actions.

承擔後果為另一個中文的形容法。它指接受自己行為的後果。

❸ Well, 接受批評 is a good example. It means accepting criticism from someone for something you have done.

接受批評為一個好的例子。它指對自己的行為接受他人的批評。

Q What are antonyms of "face the music" in English?
請問 *Face the music* 的英文反義字為何？

❶ "Pass the buck" is a good example. It is opposite to "face the music". It means avoiding responsibilities and blaming someone else.

Pass the buck 為一個好的例子。它與 face the music 相反。它指避免承擔責任，並責怪他人。

❷ You can simply say "get out of something". If you want to get out of something, it means you want to avoid something you don't want to face.

簡單來說，可以用 get out of something 來形容。假如你想 get out of something，它指避免一些你不想面對的事。

❸ Alternatively, you can just say pass responsibility to someone else.

或者，你可以說 pass responsibility to someone else。

Vocabulary 重點單字

- **punishment** *n.* 處罰

  例：If you commit a crime, you will get punishment eventually.
  假如你犯罪的話，最後還是會受到處罰。

- **complaint** *n.* 抱怨

  例：Andy has received a complaint from his neighbour about the noise.
  Andy 從他的鄰居那邊收到一個噪音的抱怨。

- **grin** *v.* 露齒笑

  例：I guess Judy had a good day because she had a grin on her face.
  我猜 Judy 有著愉快的一天，因為她一整天都露齒笑。

- **bear** *v.* 忍受

  例：Susan can't bear being lonely. She always goes out with friends.
  Susan 無法忍受孤單一整天。她總是跟朋友們出去玩。

- **orchestra pit** *n.* 樂池

  例：Richard is performing in the orchestra pit.
  Richard 在樂池裡表演著。

- **regiment** *n.* 軍隊的團

  例：A disgraceful soldier has been kicked out from his regiment.
  一位不光彩的軍人被踢出他的軍團。

- **criticism** *n.* 批評

  例：Politicians usually have to accept criticism.
  政治家通常需要接受批評。

- **sow** *v.* 播種

  例：Farmers are sowing this farm with sweet potatoes.
  農夫在田裡播種地瓜。

文化巧巧說：諺語與外交相關的文化趣事

"Face the music" is a colloquial expression and common in everyday use. People often use "face the music" when they have to confront unpleasant consequences or criticism. They are usually prepared to accept criticism or punishment when they say this phrase. "Let's face it" is another simple way to describe this phrase.

There are many similar phrases to describe "face the music" in Chinese, such as 面對現實, 接受批評, 承擔後果, 勇敢面對 or 自食其果. 自食其果 is described in a figurative sense. Its literal meaning is to eat the fruit you have sown. It denotes that you have to face the consequences of your actions. These are good examples of the differences between English and Chinese phrases. You could explain their meanings and origins to your clients or friends.

Face the music 為一個口語的用法，並且廣泛地使用於日常會話中。人們通常用 Face the music 來表達當他們要面對一些不愉快的後果或批評。當使用此句，也代表他們已做好承擔批評或處罰的準備了。

中文中有許多類似的用法來形容 Face the music，像是面對現實、接受批評、承擔後果、勇敢面對，或自食其果。自食其果是以比喻的方式形容。它字面上的意思為吃自己種的果，這代表你必需承擔自己行為的後果。

這些都是中英文慣用語差異的一些例子。你可以向你的客户或朋友們解釋這些慣用語的意義及起源。

Unit 6 Take the bull by the horns 兵來將擋，水來土掩

How to use this idiom and on what occasions you can use this idiom
這句諺語你會怎麼說、能派上用場的場合

Track 31

Literally speaking, it is very dangerous to take a bull's horns and you have to be very brave to do it. So "take the bull by the horns" means facing a difficult situation fearlessly. People usually say it when they try to confront an unpleasant situation. For example, ***I know my mother won't be happy but I have to take the bull by the horns and tell her the truth.*** This idiom is similar to a Chinese proverb - 兵來將擋，水來土掩.

從字面上的意思看，取牛角是一件極危險的事，一般人需要很大的勇氣才敢這樣做。所以 Take the bull by the horns 意指無畏懼地面對困難。通常於遭遇一些不愉快的情形時使用。舉例來說，***我知道告訴我媽媽事實，她不會開心，但是我還是要勇敢面對***。這句成語與中文諺語 -兵來將擋，水來土掩相似。

Synonyms and Analysis 中西諺語應用與翻譯

The original idiom 原來怎麼說

Take the bull by the horns

Synonyms 還能怎麼翻

Face up to, confront a difficulty, face the problem, deal with a difficult problem

Explanations 中西諺語翻譯說明

There are other ways to express this idiom, such as "face up to". An example can go like this: *He has to face up to the fact that he has lost his job.* To confront a difficulty is also a good way to describe "Take the bull by the horns". When you have to face a dangerous or difficult situation, you can use "to confront a difficulty" to describe it; for example, when a manager has to make several staff redundant, he has to confront a difficulty.

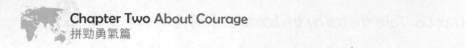

"To deal with a difficult problem" is also another way to express the same situation. However, "to deal with" also means "do business with". For instance, ***Tina works in a help desk and is used to dealing with many customers.***

有許多方法來表達這句成語，像是 Face up to。舉例來說，他需面對他已經失去工作的事實。Confront with a difficulty 也是一個形容 Take the bull by the horns 的方法。當你面臨一個艱鉅的情形時，你可以用 Confront with a difficulty 來說明。比如說，**一位經理必須裁減人員，他面臨了一個困難的處境。**

Deal with a difficult problem 也是另一個形容此情況的用法。然而，Deal with 也用在做生意上。舉例而言，***Tina 在客戶服務中心工作，已經習慣應付許多客戶。***

Analysis 中西諺語翻譯分析

"Take the bull by the horns" is used as a single phrase in sentences. You can put it after the subject. An example can go like this: *Why don't you take the bull by the horns and tell her she is not suitable for you?* To face up to and to deal with something/ somebody are used as phrasal verbs in sentences. "To confront and to face something" are used as verbs in sentences. An example can go like this: ***You have to face the problem and find a solution.***

Take the bull by the horns 在句子中當作單一片語使用。你可以將它放於主詞之後。它的應用為：*為什麼你不勇敢面對，告訴她並不適合你？* Face up to 及 deal with something/ somebody 在句子中要做為動詞片語。Confront 及 face 在句子中做為動語使用。它的應用為：***你必需面對問題，並找出解決方法來。***

Notes

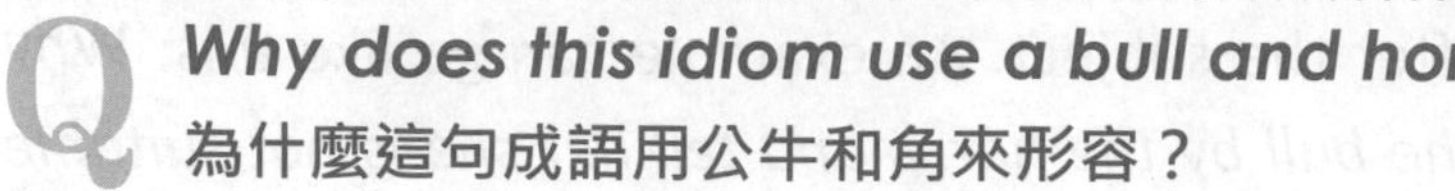

FAQ 中西文化外交交流的一問三答
Track 32

Q Why does this idiom use a bull and horns?
為什麼這句成語用公牛和角來形容？

❶ Um, it's easy to guess its definition by reading this idiom. Taking a bull's horns would put oneself in a dangerous situation. If you do so, you are going to deal with a problem openly.

嗯，其實很容易猜出它的意思。取牛角會導致一個危險的狀況。假如你這樣做了，它是意指你要公開地面對一個問題。

❷ This idiom is used in a figurative sense. Taking the bull by the horns would make the bull angry and put yourself in a dangerous situation. So it means confronting a difficulty.

這句成語是用比喻的方式來形容的。取牛的牛角會使它十分地生氣，並讓你處於一個困難的狀況。所以它代表著正視困難。

❸ Well, it's an interesting idiom. Since it's dangerous, not everyone can take the bull by the horns. Only brave people can do it. So it means doing something difficult in a determined way.

這是個趣的成語。由於十分地危險，並不是每個人都可以取牛角，只有勇敢的人才敢這麼做。所以它延伸為堅定地從事某事。

Q How do you describe this idiom in Chinese?
你要如何用中文形容這句成語？

❶ Well, there are many ways to describe it in Chinese, such as 不畏艱險. Literally speaking, it indicates someone who is not afraid of difficulties.

有許多的方法來用中文形容，像是不畏艱險。從字面上的意思來看，它是指某人不怕面對困難。

❷ You can just say 面對困難. It is similar to confronting a difficulty.

你可以說面對困難，它與 confront with a difficulty 相似。

❸ 勇敢面對 is a similar expression in Chinese. It denotes facing a problem in a brave way.

勇敢面對也是一個類似的表達方式。它意指勇於正視問題。

Q I heard there are many phrases using bulls, can you please give me some examples?

我聽說有許多慣用語使用 *Bull*，你可以舉幾個例子嗎？

❶ Like "a bull in a china shop" is a good one. It describes someone who is out of control and can damage things.

Like a bull in a china shop 為形容某人失控了，並會破壞東西。

❷ I know "Bull's-eye" from the pub game darts. If someone hits the bull's-eye, he hits the target.

我知道酒吧有射鏢遊戲 "Bull's-eye" 。假如某人擊中 bull's-eye，他命中目標。

❸ "Cash cow" generates a large profit in a business. For example, the smartphone business is this company's cash cow now. The other business units don't generate much money.

"Cash cow" 為公司賺進很多的利潤。舉例來說，智慧型手機部門現在為公司的 "Cash cow" ，其他部門並沒有為公司賺進這麼多的錢。

Vocabulary 重點單字

- **fearlessly** *adv.* 無畏懼地

例：She fought against the burglars fearlessly.
她無畏懼地與竊賊搏鬥。

- **confront** *v.* 面對

例：This is a problem we will have to confront eventually.
這是我們最終要面對的問題。

- **unpleasant** *adj.* 令人不快的

例：She has to face the unpleasant truth sooner or later. Why don't you tell her now?
她始終要面對這個不愉快的事實。為何不現在告訴她呢？

- **help desk** *n.* 客戶服務部

例：Chris works in the help desk. He has to deal with a variety of customers every day.
Chris 目前在客戶服務部工作。他每天都要應付各式各樣的客戶。

- **suitable** *adj.* 合適的

例：Graduates usually take a few years to find suitable jobs.
畢業生通常會花幾年的時間來找尋適合的工作。

- **clumsy** *adj.* 笨手笨腳的

例：He dropped books on the floor again. He is so clumsy.
他又把書丟到地下了。他真是笨手笨腳。

- **bull's-eye** *n.* 靶心

例：It's not easy to hit the bull's-eye from this distance. Well done.
從這個距離打中靶心不容易。做得好。

- **generate** *v.* 產生

例：The new harbour construction will generate thousands of jobs.
這個新的造港建設將會帶來上千個工作機會。

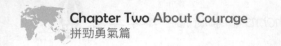

文化巧巧說：諺語與外交相關的文化趣事

There are many animal related idioms. Since every animal has a distinct character, many old English phrases use animals as examples. The literal meanings of animal related phrases are usually easy to understand. “Take the bull by the horns” is a good example.

There are many colloquial ways to describe “Take the bull by the horns”, such as facing the problem and dealing with the problem. A Chinese idiom - 初生之犢不畏虎 has a similar meaning but it’s used in a different situation. It denotes a new born calf is not afraid of a tiger because it does not know the tiger. 初生之犢不畏虎 usually describes fearless young people. This is a good example you could share with your friends or clients when you are talking about cultural differences between English and Chinese idioms.

許多的成語與動物相關。由於每個動物有著有所區分的個性，許多古老的英文成語皆以動物作為例子。動物相關成語通常也容易從字面上去理解。“Take the bull by the horns” 就是一個好的例子。

還有許多口語化的方式來敘述“Take the bull by the horns”，像是 Face the problem 及 Deal with the problem。中文成語－初生之犢不畏虎有著類似的意思，但是它是指不同的狀況。它意指由於不了解老虎的可怕，剛出生的小牛並不畏懼老虎。初生之犢不畏虎通常指無所畏懼的年輕人。當你和朋友或客戶談及中西諺語文化差異時，這是一個很好的例子。

溫馨喜樂篇

About Love and Joy

中文和英文中皆有形容言歸於好的慣用語。「化干戈為玉帛」及 *Bury the hatchet* 就是很好的例子。「化干戈為玉帛」以兵器、玉器及絲織品等來比喻化戰爭為和平，而 *Bury the hatchet* 則以埋短柄斧頭來象徵戰爭的終止。兩者來自於不同的文化背景，卻有異曲同工之妙。

Unit 01 *A friend in need is a friend indeed*
患難見真情

Unit 02 *Beauty is in the eye of the beholder*
情人眼裡出西施

Unit 03 *Bury the hatchet*
化干戈為玉帛

Unit 04 *One's cup of tea*
投其所好

A friend in need is a friend indeed
患難見真情

How to use this idiom and on what occasions you can use this idiom
這句諺語你會怎麼說、能派上用場的場合

Track 33

This proverb means that the person who helps you out when you are in trouble is a true friend. A version of this proverb can be found in the third century BC. People usually use this proverb when they realize that someone is their true friend, especially when they are in a difficult situation. For example, ***when Andrea lent me money to pay for my child's medical expenses, I realized she is a true friend. A friend in need is a friend indeed.***

這句諺語指當你遇到麻煩時，伸出援手來幫助你的朋友才是真正的朋友。這句諺語的一個版本在前三世紀中出現。一般是在認知到真正的朋友時，會使用這句諺語，尤其是在困境中。舉例來說，***當 Andrea 借錢給我支付我小孩的醫藥費時，我認知到她是真正的朋友。真是患難見真情。***

Synonyms and Analysis 中西諺語應用與翻譯

The original idiom 原來怎麼說

A friend in need is a friend indeed

Synonyms 還能怎麼翻

A friend who helps you when you are in trouble is a true friend; you can see a true friendship when you are in a difficult situation; a good friend always helps you when you are in need. A true friend is willing to help you out when you are in trouble.

Explanations 中西諺語翻譯說明

You can express this proverb in a simple way, such as a friend who helps you when you are in trouble is a true friend; you can see a true friendship when you are in a difficult situation; a good friend always helps you when you are in need or a true friend is willing to help you out when you are in trouble.

There are similar idioms describing a true friendship in Chinese, such as 患難見真情 or 士為知己者死. 患難見真情 indicates that you can only find a true friendship when you are in a difficult situation. This is a well-known phrase in China and is in everyday use. 士為知己者死 means that someone could sacrifice his life for his best friends.

你可以用簡單的方式來表達這句諺語，像是在艱困中相助的朋友才是真的朋友（A friend who helps you when you are in trouble is a true friend）、在艱困中看見真正的友誼（you can see a true friendship when you are in a difficult situation）、在需要的時候給你協助的，才是朋友（a good friend always helps you when you are in need）或 肯在你身陷困境時幫助你的，才是朋友（a true friend is willing to help you out when you are in trouble）......等。

中文成語中也有相似的例子，像是患難見真情、或是士為知己者死。患難見真情意指只能在困境中發現真摯的友情。這是在中國一句家喻戶曉的成語。士為知己者死指某人願意為他的朋友犧牲生命。

Notes

Analysis 中西諺語翻譯分析

A friend in need is a friend indeed is used as a single phrase in the sentences. For instance, ***all my friends ran away during the earthquake, but Simon helped me out and saved my life. A friend in need is a friend indeed.***

A friend in need is a friend indeed 在句子中當作單一片語使用。比如說，***當地震發生時，我的朋友們皆紛紛逃離，但 Simon 幫助我逃脫並救了我一命。真是患難見真情。***

Glossary 字彙一覽表

in need *ph.* 在危難中的	**indeed** *adv.* 真正地
willing *adj.* 樂意的	**sacrifice** *v.* 犧牲
in trouble *ph.* 在危險的處境中	**in everyday use** *ph.* 在日常生活運用
run away *v.* 逃跑	

FAQ 中西文化外交交流的一問三答 Track 34

Q *Do you have any other phrases about friendships?*
是否有其他描述友誼的慣用語？

❶ Yes, we do. "Man's best friend" is a common phrase to describe the relationship between humans and dogs.

有的，Man's best friend 是一句常用的慣用語。它用來表達人與狗之間的友誼。

❷ "Birds of a feather" is a good example. It describes people who have similar interests and get along well.

Birds of a feather 是一個好的例子。它描述有相同興趣的人們相處極佳。

❸ Well, I know "build bridges". If you try to improve relationships between two different groups or people. You can use "build bridges".

嗯，我知道 build bridges。假如你想改善兩組不同團體或人之間的關係，你可以使用 build bridges。

Please give me more examples about friend-related phrases.

請告訴我更多朋友相關慣用語的例子。

❶ Here's an example. Dogs are always loyal to their owners. That's why dogs are called man's best friend.

這裡有一個例子。狗總是對其主人忠誠。這也是為什麼狗被稱作人類最好的朋友。

❷ Sue and Andy like hiking and get along well. They're birds of a feather.

Sue 和 Andy 同樣喜愛登山，且相處甚佳。他們是臭味相投的人。

❸ There is a misunderstanding between two families. A friend of them tried to build bridges between the two families.

兩家人之間有些誤會，他們共同的朋友試著幫忙調解兩家之間的誤會。

Q Do you have any friend-related phrases in Chinese?

請問有任何朋友相關的中文慣用語嗎？

❶ Well, 豬朋狗友 is opposite to a friend in need is a friend indeed. They are friends who wouldn't help you out when you are in trouble.

豬朋狗友 跟 A friend in need is a friend indeed 是相反的。他們不會在你遭遇麻煩時，伸出援手的。

❷ Um, 竹馬之友 is a good example. They are friends in your childhood.

嗯，竹馬之友是一個好的例子。他們是你年幼時的朋友。

❸ Um, let me give you an example. 閨中密友 means girls' best friends. This phrase is commonly used.

嗯，讓我舉一個例子。閨中密友指女孩們的親密朋友。這句慣用語很常被使用。

Vocabulary 重點單字

- **friendship** *n.* 友誼

例：My brother has formed a new friendship at work.
我的弟弟在公司裡建立起一段新友誼。

- **well-known** *adj.* 出名的

例：Vicky is a well-known singer in Asia. She will have a concert in London next week.
Vicky 在亞洲為知名的歌手。她將於下週赴倫敦舉辦演唱。

- **get along** *ph.* 與……相處

例：Kate doesn't get along with her new housemate. They just had an argument.
Kate 與她的新室友相處不好。他們剛剛才發生爭執。

- **opposite** *adj.* 相反的；對立的；對面的

例：Tommy's personality is opposite to Gary's personality but they are best friends.
Tommy 的個性與 Gary 截然不同，但他們是好朋友。

- **relationship** *n.* 關係

例：It is important to keep a good relationship with your colleagues.
與同事保持良好的關係是十分地重要。

- **at odds** *ph.* 與……不合

例：She is always at odds with her mother-in-law about cleaning the house.
她總是在家庭清理方面與她的婆婆意見不合。

文化巧巧說：諺語與外交相關的文化趣事

There are many friend related phrases in ancient China and England. A friend in need is a friend indeed and患難見真情 are good examples. There are many friend related phrases to describe a variety of situations, such as build bridges and birds of a feather.

Apart from good friendships, there are phrases describing bad friendships, such as at odds with someone. When you are at odds with someone, you disagree with someone. Its example can go like this: ***David is always at odds with Maggie about their business ideas.***

豬朋狗友 is opposite to a friend in need is a friend indeed. Literally speaking, it describes friends as pigs and dogs in a figurative sense. It denotes friends who disappear when you need them.

These are interesting examples you could show your friends and clients the differences between the English and Chinese phrases.

古代中國與英國有許多跟友情相關的諺語。A friend in need is a friend indeed 及患難見真情就是一些很好的例子。不同的友情相關慣用語也適用於不同的情況，像是 Build bridges 及 Birds of a feather。

除了好的友誼之外，也有一些慣用語是形容不好的友誼，像是 At odds with someone。它是描述你與某人意見不一致。它的應用為：David 和 Maggie 總是在經營理念上意見不合。

豬朋狗友與 A friend in need is a friend indeed 意思相反。從字面上來看，它比喻朋友像豬跟狗。這是意指在你最需要朋友時，他們反而消失不見。這些皆是你可向朋友或客户說明中西慣用語差異的有趣例子。

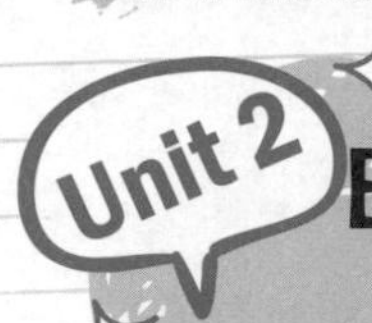

Unit 2 Beauty is in the eye of the beholder 情人眼裡出西施

How to use this idiom and on what occasions you can use this idiom 這句諺語你會怎麼說、能派上用場的場合

Track 35

Beauty is in the eye of the beholder was found in the 3rd century BC in Greece. Literally speaking, this saying indicates people judge beauty subjectively. Some people find someone or something is attractive but other people don't think so. When you find someone has a different opinion of beauty, you can use this proverb to express how you feel. For example, ***Andy is going to marry Helen. In my opinion, he can do better. I guess this is why people say beauty is in the eye of the beholder.***

Beauty is in the eye of the beholder 為前三世紀在希臘所發現的。這句諺語字面上的意思為每個人的審美觀為主觀的。有些人認為某些人或事物極具吸引力，但有些人就不這麼認為。當你發現某人跟你的審美觀有出入時，可以用這句諺語來表達你的感受。比方說，***Andy 要和 Helen 結婚了。我覺得他可以找到更好的。我想這也是為什麼人們說情人眼裡出西施。***

Synonyms and Analysis 中西諺語應用與翻譯

The original idiom 原來怎麼說

Beauty is in the eye of the beholder

Synonyms 還能怎麼翻

Love is blind, the perception of beauty is different, different people have different opinions about beauty, not everything appeals to everyone.

Explanations 中西諺語翻譯說明

"Love is blind" is similar to "Beauty is in the eye of the beholder". Love is blind describes that you find your beloved is perfect if you are in love with him or her. Love is blind is originated from the fifteenth century. It did not become so popular until it appeared in Shakespeare's plays. You can also describe this saying in a simple way, such as the perception of beauty is different, different people have different opinions about beauty or not everything appeals to everyone.

Interestingly, this saying is very close to a Chinese phrase called 情人眼裡出西施. It means lovers always think their beloved are beautiful. It is commonly used to describe the concept of beauty is not objective from the eyes of lovers.

"Love is blind" 跟 "Beauty is in the eye of the beholder" 極為相似。Love is blind 形容在情人的眼中，心愛的人永遠是完美的。Love is blind 原本源自於十五世紀。在出現於莎士比亞的戲劇前默默無聞。但被莎士比亞引用於戲劇後，Love is blind 變得很受歡迎。你也可以用簡單的方式來描述這句慣用語，像是對美的觀感是不同的（Perception of beauty is different）、對美的看法人人不同（different people have different opinions about beauty），或者是 不是每樣都吸引人（not everything appeals to everyone）。

有趣的是，這句慣用語非常接近中文的情人眼裡出西施。它指的是情人們總是認為他們心愛的人是美麗的。這句很常用在形容在情人們的眼中，美的定義是不客觀的。

Notes

Analysis 中西諺語翻譯分析

"Beauty is in the eye of the beholder" and "love is blind" are used as single phrases in sentences. For instance, ***Judy: My best friend is going to marry Ricky. To be honest, I don't really like him because he is dishonest and not even attractive. Rose: Love is blind.***

"Beauty is in the eye of the beholder" 及 "love is blind" 在句子中當作單一片語使用。舉例來說，***Judy：我最好的朋友要跟 Ricky 結婚了。老實說，我認為他很不誠實，也不特別吸引人。Rose：愛情是盲目的。***

beholder *n.* 觀看者	**blind** *adj.* 盲目的
Shakespeare 莎士比亞	**play** *n.* 戲劇
concept *n.* 想法	**objective** *adj.* 客觀的
commonly *adv.* 通常地	**lover** *n.* 戀人

FAQ 中西文化外交交流的一問三答 Track 36

Q ***Do you have other beauty-related phrases?***
請問還有其他美麗相關的慣用語嗎？

❶ Yes, we do. "Beauty is only skin deep" is a good example. This proverb denotes beautiful appearance is superficial.

有的，Beauty is only skin deep 是一個好的例子。這句話表示外在的美麗是膚淺的。

❷ Um, "a thing of beauty is a joy forever". It means the happiness from beautiful things lasts longer than beautiful things themselves.

嗯，A thing of beauty is a joy forever。從美麗事物中所獲得的快樂更勝過美麗事物本身。

❸ I know "as pretty as a picture". It simply means very pretty.

我知道 As pretty as a picture。它表示像風景一樣漂亮，即如詩如畫。

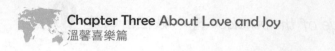

Could you please give me some examples of beauty-related phrases?

請問你可以舉 更多美麗相關慣用語的例子嗎？

❶ Of course. You can say young people care about appearance but they will find out beauty is only skin deep when they are older.

當然。你可以說許多年輕人重視外表，但他們年長時才發現外在的美麗是膚淺的。

❷ Here is an example. I enjoy taking scenery pictures and posting them on my blog. A thing of beauty is a joy forever.

這個有個例子。我喜歡拍風景照並上傳至我的部落格。從美麗事物中所獲得的快樂更勝過美麗事物本身。

❸ Um, let me think. The café next to the beach is as pretty as a picture.

嗯，讓我想想。在海邊的咖啡廳如詩如畫。

Q ***What is the difference between "beauty is in the eye of the beholder" and "love is blind"?***

"Beauty is in the eye of the beholder" 跟 "love is blind" 有什麼不同呢？

❶ Well, when you are in love with someone, you think he or she is perfect. This is why people say love is blind.

嗯，當你和某人相戀時，你認為他完美無缺。這也是人們說愛情是盲目的。

❷ "Beauty is in the eye of the beholder" often describes beauty is not objective. It's hard to have the same idea of beauty.

"Beauty is in the eye of the beholder" 通常表達美麗不是客觀的。對美的看法很難一樣。

❸ They are both ancient phrases but "love is blind" appeared in Shakespeare's plays and had been widely used.

這兩句皆源自於古代的慣用語，但是 Love is blind 出現於莎士比亞的戲劇中，並廣泛地被運用。

Vocabulary 重點單字

- **attractive** *adj.* 有吸引力的

  例：After they found a better deal, this offer wasn't attractive to them anymore.
  當他們找到一個更好的交易後，這個開價對他們已不再具有吸引力了。

- **perception** *n.* 看法

  例：Famous people usually do a lot of charitable works to change the public's perception.
  知名人士通常會做很多的慈善活動，以改變大眾對他們的觀感。

- **appeal to** *v.* 有吸引力；引起興趣

  例：This tourist attraction is designed to appeal to international tourists.
  這個觀光景點為針對國際遊客所設計的。

- **originate** *v.* 來自

  例：Paper originated from China and is widely used.
  紙源自於中國，並已廣泛地被運用。

- **superficial** *adj.* 表面的

  例：This shop is superficially attractive but they don't have any good products.
  這個商店表面上很具吸引力，但他們並沒有什麼好的產品。

- **beloved** *n.* 心愛的人

  例：When he sees his beloved, his attitude changes completely.
  當每見到他心愛的人時，他的態度完全轉變。

- **point of view** *n.* 觀點、看法

  例：From his point of view, this investment won't make much money.
  從他的觀點來看，這個投資並不能賺什麼錢。

文化巧巧說：諺語與外交相關的文化趣事

Beauty is in the eye of the beholder is a commonly used saying to express how different people have different views of beauty, especially for lovers' views of beauty. It is often used as a contrast saying two different ideas of beauty. For example, if you have negative views of someone's idea, you can use this proverb. You can also say "love is blind" in another way but it has slightly different meaning. It denotes a person can't find imperfections in his beloved from his point of view.

This is similar to a popular Chinese phrase- 情人眼裡出西施. It was mentioned in a well-known Chinese novel - 紅樓夢 (Dream of the Red Chamber). It indicates that you believe your beloved is beautiful if you are in love with him or her. What other people think doesn't matter.

These are examples of the differences between English and Chinese phrases that you can show your friends or clients.

Beauty is in the eye of the beholder 為一句被廣泛使用的諺語，主要用來表達每個人的審美觀皆不同。特別是針對情人們的審美觀。這句通常用來比較兩個不同的審美觀。舉例來說，假如你對某人有負面的想法，你可以使用這句諺語。或者也可以用"*Love is blind*"來表達，但它的定義稍微不同。它意指某人無法從其心愛的人身上發現不完美的地方。

這也與中文的情人眼裡出西施不謀而同。情人眼裡出西施曾於經典中國文學－紅樓夢出現過。它意指你認為你心愛的人為美麗的，就是美麗的。他人怎麼認為皆無所謂。這也是你可以向你的朋友或客户介绍的一些中西諺語文化差異的例子。

Bury the hatchet
化干戈為玉帛

How to use this idiom and on what occasions you can use this idiom
這句諺語你會怎麼說、能派上用場的場合

Track 37

Bury the hatchet was originally from an American Indian custom. When the leaders of Indian tribes bury the hatchet, it indicates it reaches a peace agreement. Therefore, "bury the hatchet" means stopping an argument and becoming friends. This is very similar to Chinese idioms - 化干戈為玉帛 or 前嫌盡釋.

Bury the hatchet 來自於一個美洲印地安人的習俗。當印地安部落的領袖埋起短柄斧時，意指他們達成一個和平協議。因此，Bury the hatchet 指言歸和好。這也與中文的化干戈為玉帛，或前嫌盡釋十分地相似。

Synonyms and Analysis 中西諺語應用與翻譯

The original idiom 原來怎麼說

Bury the hatchet

Synonyms 還能怎麼翻

Make up, stop a quarrel, let bygones be bygones, wipe the slate clean, kiss and make up

Explanations 中西諺語翻譯說明

You can describe "bury the hatchet" in a simple way, such as "make up" or "stop a quarrel". Other similar phrases include "let bygones be bygones", "wipe the slate clean" and "kiss and make up". "Let bygones be bygones" means forget or forgive what happened in the past, especially for the unpleasant things. "Wipe the slate clean" indicates starting over and forgetting the mistakes in the past. "Kiss and make up" means that two people stops quarrelling and becomes friends again.

你也可以用簡單的方法來形容 Bury the hatchet，像是 make up 或 stop a quarrel。其他類似的用法如 let bygones be bygones、wipe the slate clean 及 Kiss and make up。Let bygones be bygones 指忘記或原諒過去所發生的一些事情，特別是一些不愉快的事。Wipe the slate clean 指重新開始及忘卻過去的錯誤。Kiss and make up 指兩人停止爭執，重新變為朋友。

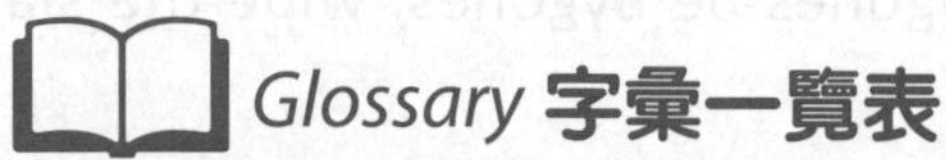

Glossary 字彙一覽表

hatchet *n.* 短柄斧	**make up** *v.* 和好
let bygones be bygones *ph.* 既往不究	**wipe the slate clean** *ph.* 一筆勾銷
kiss and make up *ph.* 使和解	**argument** *n.* 爭執
forgive *v.* 原諒	**afterwards** *adv.* 以後

Analysis 中西諺語翻譯分析

"Bury the hatchet" and "wipe the slate clean" are often put after subject in sentences and use "bury" or "wipe" as a verb. For example, *Louise and Jenny had an argument but they have buried the hatchet. Let's wipe the slate clean and forget about the argument in the past*. "Let bygones be bygone" is usually used as a single phrase in sentences. An example can go like this: ***Why can't you forgive Sam and be friends again. Let bygones be bygones.*** "Make up" is usually used as a phrasal verb in sentences. For instance, ***Mary and Nancy argue all the time but they always make up afterwards.***

Bury the hatchet 及 wipe the slate clean 通常在句中放於主詞後，以 bury 或 wipe 作為動詞使用。比方說，***Louise and Jenny 剛剛發生爭吵了，但現在已經言歸於好。我們一筆勾銷，忘掉那些過去的紛爭吧。***

Let bygones be bygone 通常在句子中作為單一片語使用。它的應用為：***為什麼你不原諒 Sam，並再成為朋友？既往不咎吧。*** Make up 通常在句子中當作動詞片語使用。例如：***Mary 和 Nancy 總是在吵架，但總是很快就和好。***

FAQ 中西文化外交交流的一問三答 Track 38

Q ***Why is this phrase relevant to a hatchet?***
為什麼這句成語跟短柄斧有關呢？

❶ A hatchet is a small axe and is used as a tool or a weapon by the American Indians in the olden days. Therefore, "bury the hatchet" denotes stopping an argument.

Hatchet 為一種小型的斧頭，在過去被美洲印地安人當作工具或武器使用。因此，埋短柄斧意味著言歸於好。

❷ Well, this is from an American Indian tradition. Hatchet indicates a weapon, so "bury the hatchet" means to stop fighting.

這是北美印地安人的一個傳統。短柄斧象徵武器，所以埋短柄斧指停止戰爭。

❸ This phrase is used in a figurative sense. "Bury the hatchet" originally means to end a war but it also indicates to stop a quarrel.

這句慣用語是用比喻的方式形容。Bury the hatchet 指結束一場戰爭，但也可以形容停止爭吵。

Q Do you have similar phrases in Chinese?
在中文是否有類似的成語？

❶ Yes, we do. You can also say "化干戈為玉帛". 干戈 means weapons and it is usually indicates wars. 玉帛 means jade and silk products, which are precious objects and often used as gifts in ancient China. So this phrase means make peace.

有的。你可以說 "化干戈為玉帛" 。干戈指的是武器，也通常指戰爭。玉帛為玉及絲製品，象徵著珍貴的物品，在古代的中國通常作為禮品使用。因此，化干戈為玉帛象徵和平。

❷ Well, there are many ways to describe "bury the hatchet" in Chinese. 言歸和好 is a good example. It means to end a quarrel and become friends.

有許多方式可形容 "Bury the hatchet" 。言歸和好就是一個很好的例子。它指的是停止爭吵並成為朋友。

❸ 前嫌盡釋 is relevant to "bury the hatchet". It means forgetting about unhappy things that happened in the past.

前嫌盡釋跟 "Bury the hatchet" 相關。它意味著忘記過去所發生的不愉快事情。

Q When can you use "bury the hatchet" and "wipe the slate clean"?

何時用 *Bury the hatchet*？何時用 *Wipe the slate clean*？

❶ Well, you usually use "bury the hatchet" when you try to settle quarrels. You usually use "wipe the slate clean" when you try to forget about bad experiences in the past.

當你結束一場紛爭時，通常會用 Bury the hatchet。當你試著忘卻過去的一些不好的經驗時，通常會用 Wipe the slate clean。

❷ When you want to stop an argument with someone, you can say "let's bury the hatchet and be friends.".

當你與某人停止爭執時，你可說：「我們不要吵了，和好吧。」（Let's bury the hatchet and be friends.）。

❸ When you try to forget about unpleasant experiences in the past and start over, you can say let's "wipe the slate clean and start a new business.".

當你試著要忘記過去的一些不愉快經驗並重新來過時，你可以說：「讓過去的一筆勾銷，我們從新開始新事業吧。」（Let's wipe the slate clean and start a new business.）。

Vocabulary 重點單字

- **agreement** *n.* 同意；協議

例：Two companies have reached an agreement to work together. 兩間公司達成協議，並共同合作。

- **quarrel** *n.* 爭吵

例：Maggie often quarrelled with her family over money issues. Maggie 常常與她的家人在金錢問題上爭執。

- **start over** *v.* 重新開始

例：Linda's professor wasn't happy with her report and made her start it over.
Linda 的教授不滿意她的報告，並要求她重交。

- **tribe** *n.* 部落

例：Many native American and Canadian tribes used to live in this area.
許多美國及加拿大原住民部落曾經住在這個區域。

- **precious** *adj.* 珍貴的

例：This is a precious memory for Amy. She won't forget about it.
這對 Amy 來說是一個珍貴的回憶。她不會輕易忘記的。

- **axe** *n.* 斧

例：The American Indians used to use axes as weapons.
美洲印地安人曾經使用斧頭作為武器。

- **signify** *v.* 表示；意味著

例：This ancient character signifies happiness.
這個古字意味著快樂。

- **slate** *n.* 石板

例：Slates are good construction materials for roofs.
石板為建造屋頂的良好建材。

文化巧巧說：諺語與外交相關的文化趣事

Bury the hatchet derived from a Native American custom. Interestingly, ancient Chinese has the same phrase to express the same situation. However, due to cultural differences, they used different objects to describe these phrases.

"Bury the hatchet" used a small axe as an example to signify the end of war. "化干戈為玉帛" used jade and silk products as examples to signify peace. Both Bury the hatchet and 化干戈為玉帛 indicate the end of wars originally but they also mean the end of quarrels nowadays. It is interesting that these phrases are used in a figurative sense. You can mention this point when you talk to your friends or clients.

Bury the hatchet 源自於一個美洲印地安人的習俗。有趣的是，古代的中國也有類似的說法來表達這種情況。然而，基於文化差異，中文和英文分別以不同的物品來形容。

Bury the hatchet 使用小形斧頭作為例子，並象徵著戰爭結束。而化干戈為玉帛則使用玉及絲製品作為例子，並象徵著和平。Bury the hatchet 及化干戈為玉帛原本皆意味著結束戰爭，但現在也可象徵停止爭吵。有趣的是，這些慣用語同時使用比喻的方式來形容。你可以向你的朋友或客户提及這個共通點。

One's cup of tea
投其所好

How to use this idiom and on what occasions you can use this idiom
這句諺語你會怎麼說、能派上用場的場合

Track 39

If something is your cup of tea, it means something is your taste. When people find something is the type of thing they like, they usually use this expression. For example, ***reality shows are my cup of tea.*** You can describe one's cup of tea as 投其所好 in Chinese. Apart from the positive expression, you can also use it in a negative way, such as not my cup of tea.

假如某些事物為 your cup of tea，表示它們為你所喜愛的事物。當人們找到適合他們的事物時，通常會使用這句慣用語來表達。舉例來說，***實境秀為我所好***。你也可以用中文的投其所好來表達。除了正面的表達方式外，你也可以用負面的方式來表達，像是 not my cup of tea。

Synonyms and Analysis 中西諺語應用與翻譯

The original idiom 原來怎麼說

One's cup of tea

Synonyms 還能怎麼翻

Taste, liking, favorite, preference, first choice

Explanations 中西諺語翻譯說明

There are many simple ways to express my cup of tea in English, such as this is my taste, liking, favorite or first choice. Preference is usually used as a comparison. For example, ***my preference for houses is its convenience rather than its size.*** "Favorite" is something you most enjoyed. For instance, ***Ben's favorite drink is coffee.*** It can be used in a negative way. For example, ***math is my least favorite subject.*** They are colloquial and commonly used in daily conversation.

英語中有許多方式來表達 my cup of tea，像是 this is my taste、liking、favorite 或 first choice。Preference 通常用來比較。舉例來說，***我注重房子的便利性，而非它的大小***。Favorite 則為你最喜愛的事物。比比如說，***Ben 最喜歡的飲料為咖啡***。它也可以負面的方式表達。比如說，***數學為我最不喜歡的科目***。這些皆為口語的用法，並實用於日常生活中。

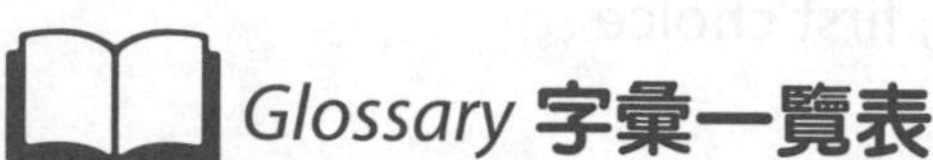

taste *n.* 愛好	**liking** *n.* 喜愛
first choice *n.* 第一選擇	**comparison** *n.* 比較
convenience *n.* 便利	**subject** *n.* 科目
negative *adj.* 負面的	**university** *n.* 大學

Analysis 中西諺語翻譯分析

Taste, liking, preference and first choice are used as nouns in sentences. Examples can go like this: ***Kevin has a taste for art. Una has a liking for black coffee. Studying Tourism is my first choice in university.*** Favorite is used as an adjective in sentences. An example can go like this: *What is your favorite movie?*

Taste、liking、preference、和 first choice 皆在句子中作為名詞使用。*它們的例子如下：**Kevin 喜愛藝術。Una 喜歡喝黑咖啡。選讀觀光科系為我在大學的第一志願***。Favorite 則在句子作為形容詞使用。舉例來說，你*最喜歡的電影為何？*

Notes

FAQ 中西文化外交交流的一問三答 Track 40

Q ***How do you describe one's cup of tea in Chinese?***
請問如何用中文來形容*One's cup of tea*？

❶ Well, there are many colloquial words in Chinese, such as 所喜愛的 or 合某人的意.

中文中有許多口語化的表達方式，像是所喜愛的或合某人的意。

❷ 投其所好 is a good example. It means someone finds something pleasing.

投其所好為一個好的例子。它指某人覺得某事為合意的。

❸ You can say 合得來. It means something is suitable for someone.

也可以用合得來形容。它指某事對某人為合適的。

Q Do you know any tea-related phrases?
請問有任何關於茶的慣用語嗎？

❶ Well, "not for all the tea in China" is an interesting expression. This phrase means even if someone gives you all the tea in China as a reward, it can't make you feel motivated and do anything. Since China was well-known to produce a large quantity of tea in the olden days, people used this fact and referred to it as something that is "one of the best or one of the kind".

Not for all the tea in China 為一個有趣的例子。這句慣用語表示即使某人給你全中國所有的茶作為獎賞，你仍然不為所動。由於中國在過去生產大量的茶，人們引用這個事實作為例子，並用此意指某物是最好的。

❷ I know "tea and sympathy". People usually say it to someone who is upset.

我知道 tea and sympathy。通常對心裡難過的人說這句話。

❸ "Tempest in a teapot" is a tea-related phrase. It means someone is overreacted for an unimportant thing. British people say "storm in a teacup".

Tempest in a teapot 為一句跟茶相關的慣用語。它指某人對一件不重要的事情反應過度。英式用法為 Storm in a teacup。

Q Could you give me examples of tea-related phrases?

請問你可以舉更多關於茶慣用語的例子嗎？

❶ Here is an example. I would not sell my mother's house for all the tea in China.

這裡有個例子。無論得到多高的報酬，我也不會賣我媽媽的房子。

❷ Here is an example for tea and sympathy. She has just lost her father. All you could do is to give her tea and sympathy.

這裡有一個關於 Tea and sympathy 的例子。她剛剛失去了她的父親，你可以做的就是給她安慰。

❸ For tempest in a teapot, you can say: This lawsuit was just a tempest in a teapot.

關於 Tempest in a teapot，可以說：這個訴訟只是小題大作。

Vocabulary 重點單字

- **reality show** *n.* 實境秀

  例：Reality shows is a new type of TV shows and has been very popular since it is created.
  實境秀為一種新的電視節目。自從發明以來，廣受歡迎。

- **preference** *n.* 偏好

  例：Which is your preference for breakfast, bread or cereal?
  你的早餐偏好為何？麵包、或是穀片？

- **tourism** *n.* 觀光

  例：Tourism is becoming an important industry in most countries. 觀光業在大部分的國家逐漸成為一個重要的產業。

- **even if** *conj.* 即使

  例：Even if it is free of charge, I don't want to go to this restaurant. 即使不收費，我也不想去這間餐廳。

- **reward** *n.* 報答

  例：My company offered a reward for the sales person who makes the most sales revenue.
  我的公司提供獎賞給業績最好的業務員。

- **sympathy** *n.* 同情

  例：He has no sympathy for criminals.
  他對罪犯沒有同情心。

- **overreacted** *adj.* 反應過度

  例：She has overreacted to this issue. It isn't as bad as she thinks.
  她對這件事反應過度。這並不是像她所想像的這麼糟。

- **tempest** *n.* 暴風雨

  例：This plane's schedule has been affected by a tempest.
  這架飛機的航班被暴風雨所影響了。

文化巧巧說：諺語與外交相關的文化趣事

One's cup of tea is a colloquial expression and can be used in both positive and negative ways. The negative expression is more often used in conversation nowadays. People usually say it to express something is not the type of thing they prefer.

Apart from one's cup of tea, there are many tea-related phrases in English. "Not for all the tea in China" was mentioned in an article in the early twentieth century in Australia. Since China produced a large quantity of tea at that time, people used this fact to describe nothing can change their mind even if they receive all the tea in China. You can also describe it as "not at any price" in English. 無論如何 is a similar expression to "not for all the tea in China" in Chinese. Apart from learning these phrases, you can also know their facts, history or culture in the past. Not for all the tea in China is a good example.

One's cup of tea 為一個口語的用法，並且可用在正面及負面的表達方式。負面的表達方式較常用在日常會話中。人們通常用此句來表達某些事物並不是他們所喜愛的。

除了 One's cup of tea 之外，英語中也有許多與茶相關的慣用語。Not for all the tea in China 曾於二十世紀初時被提及於一篇澳洲的文章中。由於過去中國生產大量的茶，人們使用這個例子來描述即使他們收到中國的茶，也不會改變心意。在英語中也可以稱為 not at any price。"無論如何"則是中文中一個類似 not for all the tea in China 的慣用語。除了學習這些慣用語外，也可藉此了解過去的事實、歷史、及文化。Not for all the tea in China 就是一個很好的例子。

中西方文化溝通篇

About Cultural Communication

中文的「開門見山」為形容一開始就進入主題。英文中也有類似的表達方法嗎？*Cut to the chase* 為形容「開門見山」的好例子。它原指剪輯電影到精采的部分，引申為切入正題。與老外溝通時，也能提及這個中西文化的共通之處喔！

Unit 01 *Flogging a dead horse*
徒勞無功；白費功夫

Unit 02 *In the nick of time*
及時趕到

Unit 03 *Pass the buck*
推卸責任

Unit 04 *Take something with a pinch of salt*
半信半疑

Unit 05 *Up in the air*
懸而未決

Unit 06 *Alive and kicking*
生龍活虎

Unit 07 *Cut to the chase*
開門見山

Unit 08 *Down in the dumps*
鬱鬱寡歡

Unit 09 *In the doghouse*
麻煩大了

Unit 10 *Up the creek without a paddle*
處於困境

Flogging a dead horse
徒勞無功；白費功夫

How to use this idiom and on what occasions you can use this idiom
這句諺語你會怎麼說、能派上用場的場合

Track 41

"Flogging a dead horse" means you're wasting time and energy on something which is unlikely to succeed. This phrase is also called "beating a dead horse", which appeared in the nineteenth century. People usually use this phrase when they believe something is pointless and it is not worth doing. For example, ***David is flogging a dead horse studying an ancient language.*** This phrase is also similar to Chinese idioms - 徒勞無功 or 白費功夫.

On the other hand, flogging a dead horse can also mean someone is incessantlyg talking about hopeless topics. This definition is less commonly used than the previous one. For example, ***my grandmother hates young people who don't follow tradition. She is just flogging a dead horse.***

Flogging a dead horse指浪費時間及精力在一些不可能會成功的事物上。這個慣用語也稱為 beating a dead horse。Beating a dead horse 於十九世紀時出現於書本裡。一般人用此句來表達一些徒勞無功的事物。比如說，***David 在學一個古老的語言，只是在白費力氣而已***。這句慣用語與中文的徒勞無功，或白費功夫非常的相似。

在另一方面來看，flogging a dead horse 也可以用在一直討論一些沒希望的話題上。這個解釋較上一個解釋少使用。舉例來說，***我的祖母討厭年輕人不遵守傳統的規範。她只是在白費力氣而已***。

Notes

Synonyms and Analysis 中西諺語應用與翻譯

The original idiom 原來怎麼說

Flogging a dead horse

Synonyms 還能怎麼翻

Beating a dead horse, pointless, hopeless, fruitless, unnecessary, useless, futile, harp on, dwell on

Explanations 中西諺語翻譯說明

As mentioned before, flogging a dead horse has two definitions. If its meaning is wasting time and energy on something which is unlikely to succeed, it is similar to pointless, hopeless, fruitless, unnecessary and useless. If its meaning is to keep talking about hopeless topics, it is similar to "harp on" or "dwell on".

如前述，flogging a dead horse 有兩個解釋。假如它指浪費時間及精力在一些不可能會成功的事物上時，它與 pointless, hopeless, fruitless, unnecessary 及 useless 相似。假如它指一直討論些沒希望的話題上，那麼它與 harp on 或 dwell on 相似。

Analysis 中西諺語翻譯分析

Flogging a dead horse is usually put after verbs in sentences. For example, *I'm afraid you are just flogging a dead horse by sending your proposal to them again. They won't approve it.* Pointless, hopeless, fruitless, unnecessary and useless are used as adjectives in sentences. Examples can go like this: ***It is pointless to continue this project without any budget. It is hopeless to expect any survivors from this earthquake.***

"Harp on" is used as a phrasal verb in sentences. It usually comes with about. An example can go like this: ***Linda likes harping on about the same topic all the time.*** "Dwell on" is also used as a phrasal verb in sentences. For instance, ***stop dwelling on the past. It is too late to change anything.***

Flogging a dead horse通常於句中置於動詞之後。舉例來說，*你再次把提案寄給他們只是白費力氣而已*，***他們不會通過這個提案的***。Pointless、hopeless、fruitless、unnecessary及useless在句中作為形容詞使用。它們的應用為：***在沒有任何預算的情形下，繼續進行這個專案只是白費功夫。在這場地震中見到任何的倖存者是毫無希望的。***

Harp on 在句中是作為片語動詞使用。它通常跟隨著about。它的應用為：***Linda總是喜歡喋喋不休地談相同的話題。Dwell on也是在句中作為片語動詞使用。舉例來說，別老是談論過去，現在也太晚去改變什麼了。***

FAQ 中西文化外交交流的一問三答 Track 42

Q ***How do you describe "Flogging a dead horse" in Chinese?***

如何用中文形容 *Flogging a dead horse* 呢？

❶ Well, you can say 白費功夫 in Chinese. It means wasting a lot of energy on something but you still get nothing.

你可以說白費功夫。它意指浪費很多精力在某件事情上，但還是一無所獲。

❷ Um, 徒勞無功 indicates that you waste a lot of time on something but it doesn't work.

嗯，徒勞無功表示花了很多時間在某事上，但還是不成功。

❸ 徒費脣舌 is another way to describe "flogging a dead horse" but it is slightly different. It means you're wasting a lot of time talking or persuading someone but it doesn't work.

徒費脣舌是另一個形容 Flogging a dead horse 的成語，但它稍微不同。徒費脣舌指浪費時間談論或說服某人，但還是無功而返。

Q I know "harp on" means incessantly talking about hopeless topics. How do you describe it in Chinese?

我知道 Harp on 指持續談論某個無希望的話題。該如何用中文形容呢？

❶ Let me think. It is similar to 喋喋不休 in Chinese. It describes someone who keeps talking and won't stop.

讓我想想。它與喋喋不休相似。它形容某人一直講不停。

❷ 嘮嘮叨叨 is a good example. It indicates to keep nagging all the time.

嘮嘮叨叨是一個好的例子。它表示嘮叨地唸個不停。

❸ 刺刺不休 is another way to describe this phrase in Chinese but it is less commonly used than the previous two examples.

刺刺不休是另一個形容法，但它較先前兩個例子少用。

Q What kind of situations do you use pointless, fruitless and hopeless respectively?

請問在什麼情況下可使用 *Pointless*、*fruitless* 及 *hopeless* 呢？

❶ Well, pointless indicates something which is meaningless. So you can say borrowing money to pay your credit card bill is pointless.

Pointless 意指無意義的事物。比如說，借錢還信用卡債是無意義的。

❷ Fruitless often means something that is unsuccessful or unproductive. When you attempt to do something for a long time but are unsuccessful, you could use this word.

Fruitless 指一些不成功或沒有效益的事情。當你試著做某事很久，但是一直不成功時，可以用此字來形容。

❸ Hopeless simply means no hope or impossible. If you have been trying something over and over but there is no solution, you can say it's hopeless.

Hopeless即指沒有希望或不可能的事。假如你一直嘗試做某事，但還是沒有解決辦法時，你可以說 It's hopeless。

Vocabulary 重點單字

- **flog** *v.* 鞭打

例：If you commit a crime in some countries, you might be flogged as a punishment.
假使你在某些國家犯法，你或許會受鞭刑作為懲罰。

- **futile** *adj.* 無效的

例：I am afraid that what he attempted to do was futile.
很遺憾，但他試圖做的事是無效的。

- **survivor** *n.* 生還者

例：There were no survivors from the tsunami.
這次海嘯並沒有任何的生還者。

- **nag** *v.* 不斷嘮叨

例：My father won't stop nagging me to get a job.
我的爸爸不斷地嘮叨，要我找份工作。

- **unproductive** *adj.* 無效益的

例：I have to say this is an unproductive business trip. We didn't get an order.
我必須說這次的出差毫無效益。我們沒有任何一張訂單。

- **parliamentary** *adj.* 國會的

例：There is a parliamentary debate tomorrow. It will talk about the environmental issues.
明天有一個國會辯論會，主要要討論環境議題。

- **attempt** *v.* 企圖

例：Don't attempt to escape from jail.
請別企圖逃獄。

文化巧巧說：諺語與外交相關的文化趣事

"Beating a dead horse" appeared in a report of the British parliamentary debate in the nineteenth century. This interesting phrase is using "a dead horse" in the figurative sense and you can easily understand its literal meaning.

There are many ways to describe this phrase in Chinese, such as 白費功夫, 徒勞無功, 無濟於事, 於事無補 or 杯水車薪. These Chinese phrases indicate that it is pointless to do something. 杯水車薪 is using a cup of water and a cart of wood in the figurative sense. It denotes that a cup of water can't put out the fire coming from a cart of wood. Therefore, it means that this is a pointless action. 無濟於事 means that it doesn't really help this situation if you do it. They are interesting examples showing the cultural differences between the Chinese and English phrases. You could share them with your clients or friends when you talk to them.

Beating a dead horse 在十九世紀時出現於一份英國國會辦論會的報告裡。這個有趣的慣用語用死馬來比喻，很容易由字面的意思了解其定義。

像白費功夫、徒勞無功、無濟於事、於事無補，或杯水車薪等皆可用來形容 Flogging a dead horse。這些中文成語意指做一些無意義的事情。杯水車薪以一杯水及一車木柴來比喻。意指一杯水無法撲滅一車木柴所引起的大火。因此，它指這是個無意義的舉動。無濟於事表示即使你這麼做了，對事情也沒有任何幫助。這都是展現東西方文化差異的一些例子。當你和客戶及朋友對談時，可以與他們分享。

In the nick of time 及時趕到

How to use this idiom and on what occasions you can use this idiom 這句諺語你會怎麼說、能派上用場的場合

Track 43

In the nick of time indicates at the last minute. It usually comes with arrive, save or get there. For example, ***Susan arrived at the airport in the nick of time. Otherwise, she would have missed her flight.*** The nick was a notch, which was used on the tally sticks in the past. It indicates precision. In the nick of time is similar to a Chinese phrase -及時趕到. "Pudding time" was another similar expression in the sixteenth century. Pudding was not served as a dessert at that time. It was served first as a savoury dish in the beginning of the meal. When someone arrived at the pudding time, it means that he or she arrives in time to eat the meal. However, when pudding became a dessert over time, this expression became unsuitable.

In the nick of time 指及時。它通常與arrive、save 或者 get there併用。舉例來說，***還好Susan及時趕到，否則她會錯過班機***。Nick 在古代為計數棒上的刻痕，它代表著精確。In the nick of time 與中文的及時趕到相似。Pudding time 為十六世紀時的一個相似用法。Pudding 當時並不是甜點。它為餐點的第一道有鹹味的菜。當某人在 Pudding time抵達用餐時，它意指他及時抵達以享用餐食。然而，隨著時間變化，pudding 漸漸變為一道甜點，這個表達方式變得不適用。

Synonyms and Analysis 中西諺語應用與翻譯

The original idiom 原來怎麼說

In the nick of time

Synonyms 還能怎麼翻

At the eleventh hour, get in under the wire, at the last minute, just in time

Explanations 中西諺語翻譯說明

There are many ways to describe this phrase, such as at "the eleventh hour" and "get in under the wire". Some examples can go like this: ***The meeting was called off at the eleventh hour. I got in under the wire just before the shop closed.*** You can also express this phrase in a simple way, such as at the last minute or just in time.

有許多的方法可以形容 In the nick of time，像是 at the eleventh hour 及 get in under the wire。它的例子為：***會議在最後一刻被取消了。我在商店關門前的最後一刻進去了。***你也可以用簡單的方法來形容 in the nick of time，如 at the last minute 或者是 just in time。

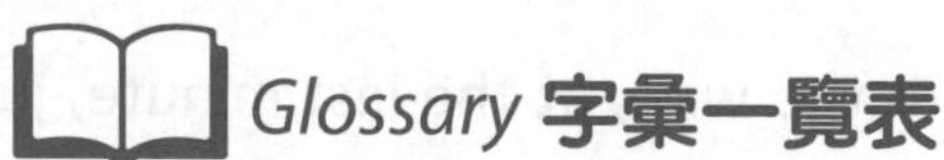

Glossary 字彙一覽表

at the eleventh hour 在最後的時刻	**under the wire** 在最後關頭
at the last minute 在最後一刻	

Analysis 中西諺語翻譯分析

At the eleventh hour is often used as a single phrase at the end of sentences. You can also use "eleventh hour" as a noun. For example, *this is an eleventh hour decision*. Get in under the wire is put after subjects in sentences. For instance, ***the lesson is about to start. Tom got in just under the wire.*** At the last minute is often put at the end of sentences. An example can go like this: ***She always prepares for her exams at the last minute.***

Just in time is used as a single phrase in sentences. An example can go like this: ***Sue arrived at the wedding venue just in time. This is the last train before Christmas. He caught the last train just in time.***

At the eleventh hour 通常做為單一片語置於句尾。也可以將 eleventh hour 當作名詞。舉例來說，***這是最後的決定（This is an eleventh hour decision.）***。Get in under the wire 在句子中置於主詞之後。例如：***這堂課即將要開始了，Tom 在最後一刻進來***。At the last minute 通常置於句尾。它的例子為：***她總是在最後一刻才準備考試***。Just in time 在句中作為單一片語使用。舉例來說：***Sue 及時趕到婚禮場地。這是聖誕節前的最後一班列車。他及時搭上了最後一班列車。***

FAQ 中西文化外交交流的一問三答 Track 44

Q *What kind of situations do you usually use at the last minute, in the nick of time and get in under the wire?*

在什麼情況可使用 *at the last minute*、*in the nick of time* 及*get in under the wire*？

❶ At the last minute is usually used for meeting or travel cancellations. If a flight is unexpectedly cancelled, you can say my flight was cancelled at the last minute.

At the last minute 通常用於取消會議、或旅遊。假如航班無預期地被取消了，你可以說航班在最後一刻被取消了。

❷ Well, "save someone in the nick of time" means someone is saved before it is too late.

Save someone in the nick of time 用來表示某人在最後一刻被救出了。

❸ "Get in under the wire" is usually used when someone arrives at a place or joins something at the last minute.

Get in under the wire 通常指在最後一刻抵達某地或加入某事。

Q How do you describe "In the nick of time" in Chinese?

該如何用中文形容 *In the nick of time* 呢？

❶ Well, you can say 在最後一刻. It means at the last possible moment.

你可以說在最後一刻。它指最後的時刻。

❷ Um, 在緊要關頭 is a good example. It indicates at the critical moment in Chinese.

嗯，在緊要關頭是一個好的例子。它的中文意思為關鍵性的一刻。

❸ You can just say 及時趕上 to express this phrase. 及時趕上 is more colloquial compared to the previous two examples.

你也可以用及時趕上來表達。及時趕上比之前的例子較為口語化。

Q *I know "nick" has different definitions. Can you tell me more about nick?*

我知道 *Nick* 有很多的定義。你可以告訴我更多 *Nick* 的定義嗎？

❶ Yes, nick has many different definitions. For English slang, nick means a prison or to catch someone who commits a crime.

是的，Nick 有很多不同的定義。在英式的俚語中，Nick 指監獄，或者是犯罪被逮捕。

❷ Well, I have had my phone nicked. It means my phone has been stolen.

I have had my phone nicked。這是指我的手機被偷了。

❸ Nick means a small cut. This is relevant to the origin of in the nick of time.

Nick 也指一個小的刻痕。這也與 in the nick of time 的起源相關。

Vocabulary 重點單字

- **savoury** *adj.* 鹹的

例：Simon prefers savoury dishes. He won't order a dessert.
Simon 喜愛吃鹹食，他不會點甜點的。

- **over time** *adv.* 隨著時間

例：An ancient custom has been changed over time.
這個古老的習俗隨著時間而變化。

- **unsuitable** *ph.* 不適合

例：This area is very dangerous and unsuitable for children.
這個區域很危險，而且不適合兒童。

- **call off** *v.* 取消

例：Tomorrow's game has been called off because a typhoon is coming.
明天的比賽因颱風來臨而取消。

- **cancellation** *n.* 取消

例：This doctor's diary has been fully booked. If there are any cancellations, we will let you know.
這個醫生的預約已滿，若有任何的取消，會再通知你。

- **critical** *adj.* 關鍵的

例：Next year's election is critical for this country's future.
明年的選舉對這個國家的未來十分的關鍵。

- **just in time** *ph.* 及時

例：You arrived just in time. I was about to leave.
你及時趕到，不然我正準備走了。

- **promptly** *adv.* 立即地

例：Jessica always replies to her clients' emails promptly.
Jessica 總是立即地回覆她客戶的電子郵件。

文化巧巧說：諺語與外交相關的文化趣事

Nick has multiple definitions in English. As a noun, it means a small cut. It also indicates prison in English slang. As a verb, it means steal something or arrest someone. When in the nick of time appeared in Arthur Day's Festivals in the seventeenth century, it had the same meaning we know today. The other relevant English phrases are at the eleventh hour, get in under the wire, at the last minute or just in time.

There are many ways to describe in the nick of time in Chinese, such as 在最後一刻, 在緊要關頭, 正趕上 or 及時趕上. 及時 can also mean timely or promptly in Chinese. 在緊要關頭means at the critical moment. These examples are colloquial and in everyday use.You could let your clients or friends know there are similar phrases in both Chinese and English languages.

Nick在英文中有許多的定義。作為名詞，它表示刻痕。英文的俗語也意指監獄。作為一個動詞，它指偷東西、或逮捕某人。當In the nick of time於十七世紀出現於Arthur Day's Festivals時，它有著與現今相同的意思。其他相關的英文慣用語為at the eleventh hour, get in under the wire, at the last minute，或者是just in time。

中文中也有類似的形容法，像是在最後一刻、在緊要關頭、正趕上、或 及時趕上等。這些例子皆非常口語化，且常常被使用。你可以讓你的客户或朋友了解東西文化的共通之處。

Pass the buck
推卸責任

How to use this idiom and on what occasions you can use this idiom
這句諺語你會怎麼說、能派上用場的場合

Track 45

If you pass the buck, it means that you blame someone for a problem you should face. This phrase was originally from a poker game in the nineteenth century. When a dealer has finished his turn, he would pass the buck to the next player. People usually say this phrase when they complain someone is avoiding taking responsibility. For example, ***stop passing the buck. You know you're responsible for this problem.*** This phrase is similar to a Chinese phrase called 推卸責任.

Pass the buck指把你原本該面對的責任推卸給別人。它起源於十九世紀的撲克牌遊戲。每當發牌者結束了一局，他會將 Buck 傳給下一個玩家。人們通常於抱怨他人推托時，使用此句。舉例來說，***不要再推托了，你知道你應對這個問題負責***。這個慣用語與中文的推卸責任相似。

Synonyms and Analysis 中西諺語應用與翻譯

01 chapter
02 chapter
03 chapter
04 chapter

The original idiom 原來怎麼說

Pass the buck

Synonyms 還能怎麼翻

Blame something on someone, pass responsibility to someone else, evade responsibility, get out of

Explanations 中西諺語翻譯說明

You can describe this phrase in a simple way, such as blame something on someone, pass responsibility to someone else, evade responsibility or get out of. For example, ***Louise blamed this mistake on Susan but it was her fault. You can't evade the responsibility anymore. It is better to tell them the truth.***

Take the blame and shoulder the responsibility are opposite to pass the buck. Take the blame denotes that a person admits that he or she is responsible for a mistake. Shoulder the responsibility means taking responsibility for something.

Get out of something means give an excuse to avoid doing something. For example, some parents want their children to learn more skills, so they send their children to extracurricular lessons. However, their children usually find excuses to get out of these lessons.

可以用簡單的方式來形容 Pass the buck，像是 blame something on someone, pass responsibility to someone else, evade responsibility, 或者是 get out of。舉例說明，***Louise 責怪 Susan 犯錯，但這其實是她自已的錯。你不要再逃避責任了，最好告訴他們事實。***

Take the blame 和 shoulder the responsibility 與 pass the buck 相反。Take the blame 表示某人承認他對某失誤負責。Shoulder the responsibility 指願意承擔責任。

Get out of something 指找藉口來逃避做某些事。舉例來說，有些父母想要讓他們的孩子多學些技能，並讓他們參加課外課程。然而，他們的孩子通常找藉口來逃避參加這些課程。

Analysis 中西諺語翻譯分析

Blame, pass and evade are used as verbs and put after subjects in sentences. For example, ***Maggie usually passes her responsibility to someone else. She believes that she is always right.***

Get out of is usually used as a phrasal verb and put after subjects in sentences. An example can go like this: ***He said he was sick many times but was just making excuses to get out of gym class.***

Blame, pass 及 evade 在句子作為動詞，並置於主詞後。舉例說明：***Maggie 通常將責任推托給別人。她認為她永遠是對的。***

Get out of 通常在句中作為片語動詞，並置於主詞後。它的應用為：***他說他病了好幾次，其實他只是找藉口來逃避健身房的課程。***

FAQ 中西文化外交交流的一問三答 Track 46

Q *I know there are many phrases related to blaming. Can you please tell me more about it?*

我知道有很多跟責罵相關的慣用語。請問你可以告訴我更多的相關語嗎？

❶ Yes, blame game is a good example. When two or more parties are involved in a mistake, everyone tries to blame one another for the mistake.

好的，blame game 是一個好的例子。當兩方以上牽涉到一個錯誤，每個人試著互相責怪對方。

❷ Um, "a bad workman blames his tools" is a phrase describing a person who blames a mistake on work equipment. This phrase is commonly used in conversation.

嗯，a bad workman blames his tools 為形容某人將錯歸於他的生財工具上。這句成語很常在日常會話中使用。

❸ Well, people usually use "I don't blame you" to express understanding why others are doing things in this way.

一般人都用 I don't blame you 來表達你了解為何某人做某事。

Q Can you please give me more examples about the phrases related to blaming?

請問你可以舉更多責罵相關的例子嗎？

❶ Here is an example. Richard and Ricky are playing the blame game over the loss of an important client.

這裡有一個例子。Richard 和 Ricky 因為失去了一個大客戶，在玩互相推卸責任的遊戲。

❷ Um, I have an example for a bad workman blames his tools. My friend is a wedding photographer. He has never taken good photos and always says he needs a new camera. I don't agree with him because a good workman never blames his tools.

嗯，我有一個關於 a bad workman blames his tools 的例子。我的朋友是一個婚禮攝影師，他從未照出好的照片來，而且總是推說他需要一台好的相機。我不同意他的觀點，因為一個好的工匠不會責怪他的工具。

❸ Well, I don't blame you for not attending my birthday party. I know your child is not well.

我不怪你沒有出席我的生日派對。我知道你的孩子不舒服。

Q What can you say "pass the buck" in Chinese?
如何用中文形容 Pass the buck 呢？

❶ You can say 推卸責任 in Chinese. It indicates getting rid of responsibilities. This phrase is in everyday use.

你可以說推卸責任。它是指免除責任。這句成語很實用。

❷ Well, 不願承擔責任 is a way to express "pass the buck". It means that someone doesn't want to take responsibility for something.

可以用不願承擔責任來表達 Pass the buck。它表示某人不願對某事負責。

❸ Um, it's similar to 抵賴. It denotes that someone refuses to admit something.

嗯，它與抵賴相似。抵賴表示某人拒絕承認某事。

Vocabulary 重點單字

- **poker** *n.* 撲克牌遊戲

  例：Johnny usually plays poker with his brothers during the weekend.
  Johnny 通常於週末同他的弟弟們玩撲克牌。

- **evade** *v.* 逃避

  例：Ben has been evading the question and wouldn't talk to me.
  Ben 一直在逃避問題，不願與我對話。

- **shoulder** *v.* 承擔

  例：He didn't want to shoulder the responsibility and tried to pass the buck.
  他不願意承擔責任，並想把錯失歸給其他人。

- **dealer** *n.* 發牌者

  例：It is your turn to be the dealer.
  換你做發牌者了。

- **workman** *n.* 工匠

  例：The house is not habitable. We need to find a workman to do it up.
  這間房子無法居住。我們必須找一個工匠來整修。

- **shift** *v.* 轉嫁

  例：Stop shifting the responsibility to your subordinates.
  別再把責任推給你的下屬了。

- **responsibility** *n.* 責任

  例：Social responsibility is very important for a business.
  社會責任對一個企業而言十分地重要。

文化巧巧說：諺語與外交相關的文化趣事

Pass the buck originated from the American poker game in the nineteenth century. When a dealer finished his turn in a poker game, he passed the buck. It indicates shifting someone's responsibility to someone else. It has been widely used since it was created.

The buck stops here and take the blame are other relevant phrases. They are similar to each other but have slightly different definitions. When you say the buck stops here, it means that you will take responsibility if anything goes wrong. When you say "I'll take the blame", it indicates that you admit a mistake you have made.

There are many ways to express pass the buck in Chinese, such as 推卸責任, 推托責任, 不願承擔責任 or 不肯負責. They are colloquial and have been widely used in Chinese. It is helpful to understand the origins of phrases because it makes you learn its culture.

Pass the buck 起源於十九世紀的美國撲克牌遊戲。當發牌者結束一局時，他便將 buck 傳給下個人。這也暗示著卸下了責任，並交由下一個人。這句慣用語自從被發明後，便廣泛地被使用。

The buck stops here 及 take the blame 為其他的相關語。兩者皆相似但其定義稍微不同。當你說 The buck stops here 時，表示假使出錯的話，你會負責。當你說 I'll take the blame 時，這代表你承認一個你犯的錯誤。

有許多方法可用中文表達 pass the buck，像是推卸責任、推托責任、不願承擔責任，或不肯負責等。它們皆為口語化的用法，並且廣泛地被使用於日常會話中。了解成語的起源對於學習成語很有幫助，因為這會使你從中學習其文化。

Take something with a pinch of salt 半信半疑

How to use this idiom and on what occasions you can use this idiom 這句諺語你會怎麼說、能派上用場的場合

Track 47

Take something with a pinch of salt indicates that you believe something is not completely true. The idea behind take something with a pinch of salt was that food can be easily swallowed if you take it with a pinch of salt. This is similar to another phrase called hard to swallow. It means that it is hard to believe. People usually use take something with a pinch of salt when they think someone exaggerates something. For example, ***you need to take her words with a pinch of salt. They're not 100% true.*** This phrase is similar to a Chinese idiom called 半信半疑.

Take something with a pinch of salt 表示你不完全相信某事。Take something with a pinch of salt 的起源為假使食物與一小撮的鹽搭配，比較容易吞嚥。這與另一個慣用語 Hard to swallow 的意思相似。Hard to swallow 代表很難相信。一般人通常用 Take something with a pinch of salt 來表示誇大其詞。舉例來說，***你不能完全相信她所說的話。並不是百分之百正確***。這句慣用語和中文的半信半疑的意思不謀而合。

Synonyms and Analysis 中西諺語應用與翻譯

The original idiom 原來怎麼說

Take something with a pinch of salt

Synonyms 還能怎麼翻

Hard to swallow, hard to believe, dubious, doubtful, suspicious, sceptical

Explanations 中西諺語翻譯說明

Hard to swallow has the similar idea as the origin of take something with a pinch of salt. You can also express take something with a pinch of salt in a simple way, such as hard to believe, dubious, doubtful, suspicious or sceptical.

Hard to swallow 與 Take something with a pinch of salt 有著相似的由來。你也可以用簡單的方式來表達 Take something with a pinch of salt，比如 Hard to believe、dubious、doubtful、suspicious 或者是 sceptical。

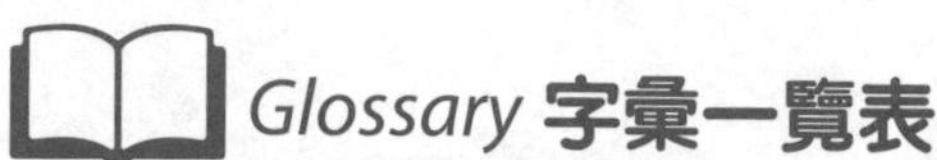

Glossary 字彙一覽表

pinch *n.* 一撮	**hard to swallow** 難以置信
doubtful *adj.* 懷疑的	**suspicious** *adj.* 可疑的
sceptical *adj.* 抱持懷疑態度的	**new recruits** *n.* 新來的人
explanation *n.* 解釋	**scientist** *n.* 科學家

Analysis 中西諺語翻譯分析

Take something with pinch of salt is usually put after subjects in sentences. An example can go like this: ***I often tell new recruits to take what Maggie says with a pinch of salt.*** Hard to swallow is usually put after verbs in sentences. For instance, ***Stephen's explanation is hard to swallow.***

Doubtful, dubious, suspicious and sceptical are used as adjectives and put after subjects in sentences. Examples can go like this: ***Una is suspicious of Tom's explanation. Many scientists remain sceptical of this study's results.***

Take something with pinch of salt 通常於句中置於主詞後。它的應用為：*我通常對新進人員說，**對 Maggie 所說的話要半信半疑**。*Hard to swallow 則於句子中置於動詞後。舉例來說，***Stephen 的解釋是難以相信的。***

Doubtful、dubious、suspicious 或者是 sceptical 於句中置於主詞後，並作為形容詞使用。例子為：***Una 對 Tom 的解釋起了疑心。許多科學家們對這份研究抱著懷疑的態度。***

FAQ 中西文化外交交流的一問三答 Track 48

Q ***How do you describe "take something with a pinch of salt" in Chinese?***

請問要如何用中文描述*Take something with a pinch of salt*呢？

❶ Well, you can say 半信半疑 in Chinese. Its literal meaning is someone believes something but also feel suspicious about it at the same time.

你也可說半信半疑。字面上的意思是某人相信某事，但同時也覺得懷疑。

❷ Um, you can also say 將信將疑. This means that it is hard to identify if it is true or not.

嗯，你可以用將信將疑來表示。這句意指很難去辨別事情的真假。

❸ 疑信參半 is a good example. Literally speaking, it indicates half trust and half suspicion, so it denotes someone who doesn't really know if something is trustworthy.

疑信參半是一個很好的例子。從字面的意思來看，它代表一半相信、一半懷疑。所以它的意思為某人並不完全知道某事的可信度。

Q What are antonyms of "take something with a pinch of salt"?

Take something with a pinch of salt 的反義字為？

❶ Well, there are many antonyms of taking with a pinch of salt, such as believable or truthful.

Take something with a pinch of salt 有許多的反義字，像是 believable、或者是 truthful。

❷ Um, "plausible" is opposite to "take with a pinch of salt". It means something is likely to be true.

嗯，plausible 與 take something with a pinch of salt 相反喔。它表示某事似乎可信。

❸ The relevant antonym is trustworthy. If you say something is trustworthy, it means it is reliable and can be trusted.

它的相關反義字為 trustworthy。假如某事為 trustworthy，它代表這件事為可靠並可相信的。

Q *What is the difference between take something with a pinch of salt and hard to swallow?*

Take something with a pinch of salt **和** ***hard to swallow*** **有什麼差別呢？**

❶ Well, if you take something with a pinch of salt, you believe something is not completely true. If you think something is hard to swallow, you think it's difficult to believe.

假如你用 take something with a pinch of salt，你覺得某事並不是完全可信。假如你用 Hard to swallow，你覺得某事難以相信。

❷ Let me give you an example of hard to swallow. My friend told me that he graduated from Cambridge University. I think it is pretty hard to swallow as he doesn't know the capital of Spain.

讓我舉一個 Hard to swallow 的例子吧。我的朋友跟我說他從劍橋大學畢業，我覺得難以相信。因為他連西班牙的首都在哪都不知道。

❸ Um, my sister likes to exaggerate all the time. I always take her words with a pinch of salt.

嗯，我的姊姊總是喜歡誇大，我對她的話都半信半疑。

Vocabulary 重點單字

- **gullible** *adj.* 輕信的

例：Sabrina is so gullible and believes everything he says.
Sabrina 很容易相信別人的。她完全相信他所說的話。

- **exaggerate** *v.* 誇大

例：Are you exaggerating? He doesn't seem so rich.
你在誇大嗎？他看起來沒有這麼的有錢。

- **dubious** *adj.* 半信半疑的

例：Susan is dubious about this traditional custom. She is not so superstitious.
Susan 對這個傳統習俗半信半疑的。她不是這麼的迷信。

- **trustworthy** *adj.* 值得信賴的

例：This website is trustworthy. You can make payment on this website.
這個網站是可信任的。你可以在這個網站付款。

- **antonym** *n.* 反義字

例：Fat is the antonym of slim.
肥胖的反義字為苗條的。

- **hook** *n.* 魚鉤

例：A fishing hook and a sinker are necessary for fishing.
魚鉤及鉛錘為釣魚時必需用的。

- **fishing** *n.* 釣魚

例：Bob usually goes fishing in a nearby river.
Bob 經常到附近的河釣魚。

- **sinker** *n.* 釋義：鉛錘

例：When you go fishing, you use a sinker to sink the line and net.
當你釣魚時，你用鉛錘將釣線及網沉入水裡。

文化巧巧說：諺語與外交相關的文化趣事

A pinch of salt was mentioned in the 77 A.D. and has been widely used since the seventeenth century. Take something with a pinch of salt is used in a figurative sense. The origin of the phrase is people believe that it is easy to swallow food with a pinch of salt in the olden days.

There are many ways to describe take something with a pinch of salt in Chinese, such as 半信半疑 or 疑信参半. These phrases indicate someone accepts a story or an explanation but he or she still remains sceptical of it. The antonym of 半信半疑 is 深信不疑. It means someone completely believes something.

If you want to describe 深信不疑 in English, fall for something hook, line and sinker is a good example. As you can see from its literal meaning, hook, line and sinker is relevant to fishing. If you fall for something hook, line and sinker, it means you completely believe something but it is not true. It is also called swallow something hook, line, and sinker.

There are many interesting stories behind these phrases. You could share them with your friends or clients.

A pinch of salt 在 77 A.D. 時被提及，並於十七世紀時被廣為使用。Take something with a pinch of salt 是用比喻的方式所表示。它的起源為古代的人們相信吃食物時，配一小撮鹽比較好吞嚥。

有許多形容 take something with a pinch of salt 的中文表達方式，如半信半疑，或疑信參半。這幾句成語是指某人接受一些說法或解釋，但還是保有懷疑的態度。半信半疑的反義字為深信不疑，它表示某人完全相信某事。

假使使用英文來表達深信不疑，fall for something hook, line and sinker 是一個好的例子。從字面上來看，hook, line and sinker 與釣魚相關。假如你 fall for something hook, line and sinker，這表示你完全相信某事，但事實上它不是真的。它也稱為 swallow something hook, line, and sinker。這些慣用語的背後擁有許多有趣的故事，你也可與你的朋友或客户分享。

Up in the air
懸而未決

How to use this idiom and on what occasions you can use this idiom
這句諺語你會怎麼說、能派上用場的場合

Track 49

If something is up in the air, it is uncertain and has not been decided yet. In the air appeared in the eighteenth century. It is often used to describe a plan, a project or a construction which is still pending. For example, ***the airport express construction is still up in the air.*** A Chinese idiom -懸而未決 is similar to this phrase.

假如某件事為Up in the air，它代表著不確定，並且尚未決定。In the air 在十八世紀時出現，它通常用來形容未定的計劃、專案，或工程。舉例來說，***機場快線工程還是不明確***。Up in the air 也與中文的懸而未決不謀而同。

Synonyms and Analysis 中西諺語應用與翻譯

The original idiom 原來怎麼說

Up in the air

Synonyms 還能怎麼翻

Pending, uncertain, undecided, unresolved, unsettled, unclear, unsure, iffy, in the balance

Explanations 中西諺語翻譯說明

In the balance is another way to describe this phrase. It usually comes with hang and is used to describe someone or something's future, especially for a critical situation. For example, ***the future of his business is hanging in the balance. He might close his business and get a job soon.***

There are many simple ways to express up in the air in English, such as pending, uncertain, undecided, unresolved, unsettled, unclear, unsure or iffy. Iffy is a colloquial word. It usually comes with about. For instance, ***Tommy is a bit iffy about studying overseas.***

In the balance 為另一個表達 up in the air 的慣用語。它通常與 hang 共用，並且用來形容某人或某事的未來，特別是指緊要的情形。比如，***他的生意狀況仍不明確，他有可能會結束營運，並且儘快找工作。***

還有許多簡易的方法來表達 up in the air，像是 pending、uncertain、undecided、unresolved、unsettled、unclear、unsure 或 iffy 等。Iffy 為較口語化的用法，它通常與 About 共用。比方說，***Tommy 還是未決定是否出國讀書。***

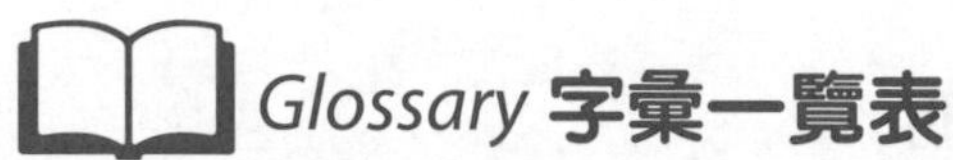

unresolved *adj.* 未解決的	**unsettled** *adj.* 未穩定的
unclear *adj.* 不明確的	**hang** *v.* 懸掛
a bit *adv.* 有一點	**critical** *adj.* 緊要的
application *n.* 申請書	

Analysis 中西諺語翻譯分析

Up in the air is often used as a single phrase and can be put after verbs in sentences. For instance, ***this contract is still up in the air. I don't think we could get it this year.***

Pending, uncertain, undecided, unresolved, unsettled, unclear, unsure, iffy are adjectives and can be put after subjects in sentences. Their examples can go like this: ***I am afraid that your application is still pending. He is still undecided about getting a job. This lawsuit remains unresolved.***

Up in the air 在句子中通常作為單一片語使用，並置於動詞後。舉例來說，***這份契約還是懸而未決。我不認為我們今年會取得。***

Pending, uncertain, undecided, unresolved, unsettled, unclear, unsure, iffy 在句中置於主詞後，並當作形容詞使用。它們的例子為：***我很遺憾你的申請書還在審核中。他還沒決定是否找份工作。訴訟尚未解決。***

FAQ 中西文化外交交流的一問三答 Track 50

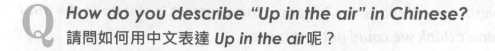

Q ***How do you describe "Up in the air" in Chinese?***
請問如何用中文表達 *Up in the air*呢？

❶ Um, let me think. You can say 懸而未決 in Chinese. It denotes something is put on hold.

嗯，讓我想想。你可以用懸而未決來表示。它指某事暫緩進行。

❷ 暫時擱置 is a good way to describe up in the air. It means something is pending now but it will be dealt with soon.

暫時擱置也是個不錯的形容法。它指某事目前暫停，但是將來會再進行。

❸ You can also say 遲疑未決. It indicates you are still considering something and still can't make a decision.

可以用遲疑未決來形容。它表示還在考慮，遲遲無法做出決定。

Q *What is the difference between "up in the air" and "in the balance"?*

***Up in the air* 和 *in the balance* 的差別為？**

❶ Well, in the balance usually indicates something or someone's future is uncertain and at risk.

In the balance 表示某事或某人的前途未卜，並存在著風險。

❷ Well, up in the air often indicates something is pending because other things have to be dealt with first.

Up in the air 通常表示因為其他事情較優先的關係，某件事需暫緩。

❸ Um, let me give you an example. My friend's company isn't a profitable business and is about to make redundancies. Hundreds of people's jobs are in the balance.

嗯，讓我舉一個例子說明。我朋友的公司營運不佳，並準備裁員。上百人的工作還懸而未決。

Q What are the antonyms of up in the air?
Up in the air 的反義字為？

❶ Um, you can simply say "finished" or "completed". They are opposite to up in the air.

嗯，簡單來說就是 Finished，或 Completed。它們與 Up in the air 的意思相反。

❷ Its antonyms include "decided", "resolved", "fixed", or "settled".

它的反義字包含 Decided、Resolved、Fixed 或 Settled。

❸ Alternatively, you can describe its antonyms as "certain" or "sure".

或者，你也可以用 Certain 或 Sure 來形容。

Vocabulary 重點單字

- **pending** *adj.* 未定的
  例：The new airport development has been pending for two years.
  新機場建設已暫停兩年了。

- **iffy** *adj.* 未確定的
  例：Judy is a bit iffy about getting that job.
  Judy 還不確定是否找工作。

- **redundant** *adj.* 被裁減的
  例：He was made redundant during the economic recession.
  他於經濟衰退期時被裁員了。

- **metaphorical** *adj.* 隱喻的
  例：This poem is written in a metaphorical way.
  這首詩以隱喻的方式描寫。

- **temporarily** *adv.* 暫時地
  例：This shop is closed temporarily for staff training.
  這間商店因員工訓練，暫時地關閉。

- **profitable** *adj.* 有盈利的
  例：Rob's business made a loss during the financial crisis and has started to become a profitable business recently.
  Rob 的公司於金融風暴時虧損，但近期開始獲利。

- **lawsuit** *n.* 訴訟
  例：David has filed a lawsuit against his former employer.
  David 向他的前雇主提出訴訟。

- **hang in the balance** *ph.* 懸而未決
  例：He had a serious car accident and stays in the intensive care unit. His life is hanging in the balance.
  他發生嚴重的車禍，目前在加護病房觀察中。他的性命懸而未決。

文化巧巧說：諺語與外交相關的文化趣事

Up in the air is described in a metaphorical way. If something is undecided, it is like something floating in the air. This is very similar to a Chinese idiom - 懸而未決. The literal meaning of 懸 is suspend and the literal meaning of 未決 is undecided. Both up in the air and 懸而未決came from similar ideas and used metaphoric expressions.

暫且擱下 is another way to express up in the air in Chinese. Compare to 懸而未決, 暫且擱下 is more colloquial. It means something is put on hold temporarily because it is less important than other tasks or can't be resolved immediately. This idiom is commonly used in conversations. This is how you can show the similarity between Chinese and English phrases to your clients and friends.

Up in the air 為用隱喻的方式形容。若某事尚未決定，就好比懸浮在空中一般。這也與中文的懸而未決不謀而同。懸的字面意思為飄浮著，而未決的字面意思為未決定的。Up in the air 及懸而未決兩者皆來自於類似的想法，並且使用隱喻的描述方法。

暫且擱下為另一個表達 Up in the air 的中文敘述方式。與懸而未決相比，暫且擱下為口語的用法。它表示某件事因為較不重要，或無法立即解決而暫緩。暫且擱下常於會話中使用。你可以向你的客户或朋友們，引述這些例子的文化共通之處。

Alive and kicking
生龍活虎

How to use this idiom and on what occasions you can use this idiom
這句諺語你會怎麼說、能派上用場的場合

Track 51

This expression appeared in the late eighteenth century and has been widely used since it was created. It describes that someone is very active or something is still popular. If it describes people, it is usually used for elderly people or someone who has just recovered his or her health. For instance, ***Joey had an operation last month. How is he now? He recovered from his operation quickly. He is alive and kicking now.*** If it describes something, it is often used in an old tradition. For example, ***the traditional opera is still alive and kicking.*** The relevant Chinese phrases are 生氣勃勃，朝氣蓬勃 or 生龍活虎.

Alive and kicking源自於十八世紀末，並自發明以來就廣為使用。它表示某人還是很活躍、或某事還是很受歡迎。假如用來形容人，它通常適用於年長人士，或者是身體剛剛復原的人。舉例來說，***Joey上個月剛剛進行了一個手術。他現在如何？他已經快速地恢復，現在可是生龍活虎呢！***假如用來形容事物，它通常適用於一個古老的傳統，比如，***傳統歌劇還是很受歡迎。****它的中文相關詞為生氣勃勃、朝氣蓬勃、或生龍活虎。*

Synonyms and Analysis 中西諺語應用與翻譯

The original idiom 原來怎麼說

Alive and kicking

Synonyms 還能怎麼翻

Alive and well, live and kicking, vigorous, well, healthy, fit as a fiddle, in the pink, in the land of the living

Explanations 中西諺語翻譯說明

There are many ways to describe alive and kicking, such as alive and well, live and kicking, fit as a fiddle, in the pink or in the land of the living. You can also express this idiom in a simple way, such as vigorous, well or healthy.

Fit as a fiddle is used in a figurative sense. A fiddle is a colloquial name for a violin. Since a violin needs to be maintained regularly in order to stay in a good condition, the phrase is used to describe a good and healthy physical condition.

Alive and kicking 有許多的形容法，像是 Alive and well、live and kicking、fit as a fiddle、in the pink 或 in the land of the living 等。簡單的形容法有 vigorous、well 或 healthy 等。

Fit as a fiddle 以比喻的方式來形容。Fiddle 為 Violin 口語的名稱。小提琴需要定期的保養，以維持它良好的狀況。因此此慣用語被用來形容一個良好及健康的狀態。

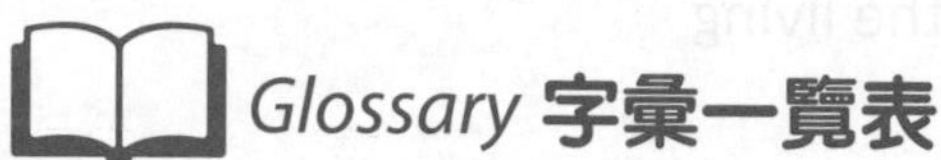

alive *adj.* 有活力的	**vigorous** *adj.* 精力充沛的
fit as a fiddle 非常健康	**maintain** *v.* 維持
regularly *adv.* 定期地	**in the pink** 容光煥發
plenty of 大量的	**physical exercise** *n.* 體能訓練

Analysis 中西諺語翻譯分析

Both fit as a fiddle and in the pink mean very health and are usually put after verbs in sentences. Examples can go like this: ***I felt as fit as a fiddle after drinking plenty of water. After a few days of rest, she is in the pink again.***

Vigorous and healthy are used as adjectives in sentences. For example, John is a vigorous young boy. You can also use vigorous to describe physical exercise. For instance, ***don't do vigorous exercise after an operation.***

Fit as a fiddle 和 in the pink 皆表示非常健康。它們通常於句中置於動詞之後。舉例說明：***我喝完大量的水後，覺得自己非常的健康。在休息幾天後，她又恢復健康了。***

Vigorous 及 healthy 於句中作為形容詞使用。比方說，***John 是一位精力充沛的青年***。也可以用 Vigorous 來形容體能訓練。例如，***別在手術後做過多的劇烈運動。***

FAQ 中西文化外交交流的一問三答 Track 52

Q ***"Alive and kicking" and "in the pink" sound interesting. Are they only used for old people?***

***Alive and kicking* 和 *in the pink*聽起來很有趣。它們只適用於老年人嗎？**

❶ No, you can use alive and kicking for people who have just recovered from a serious illness or an operation.

沒有，你可以用 Alive and kicking 來形容那些剛剛從疾病或手術復原的人。

❷ Alive and kicking can be used to describe traditional things which are still popular.

Alive and kicking 可來形容那些至今還盛行的傳統事物。

❸ Apart from being very healthy, you can also use "in the pink" to describe when a business works well. Here is an example. My uncle's company is in the pink and makes money.

除了非常健康外，你也可以用 In the pink 來描述公司營運佳。舉例來說，我叔叔的公司營運良好，並賺了很多錢。

Q Do you have similar idioms in Chinese?

中文中是否有類似的成語？

❶ Yes, we do. You can say 生氣勃勃 or 朝氣蓬勃. They are similar to vigorous.

有的。你可以說生氣勃勃，或者是朝氣蓬勃。它們與精力充沛類似。

❷ Um, 生龍活虎 is a good example. Its literal meaning is as energetic as dragons and tigers.

嗯，生龍活虎是個不錯的例子。它字面上的意思為如龍虎般地有精神。

❸ 龍騰虎躍 is another Chinese idiom using a dragon and a tiger as an example. Its literal meaning is jumping like a dragon and a tiger. It denotes as vigorous as a dragon and a tiger.

龍騰虎躍為另一個用龍和虎形容的中文成語。它字面上的意思為像龍虎一般地跳躍。它暗示著如龍虎般充滿朝氣。

Q Can you give me more examples about these phrases?

請問你可以舉更多相關的例子嗎？

❶ Here is an example. Most old people are as fit as a fiddle nowadays.

這裡有個例子。現今大部分的老年人皆非常的健康。

❷ One of my friends has just recovered from a serious illness. He is alive and well now.

我的一位朋友剛剛從疾病中復原了。他現在如生龍活虎般地健康。

❸ Let me show you an example. There is a vigorous opposition to the construction of a nuclear power plant.

讓我舉一個例子。新核能發電廠的興建案遭到強烈的反對。

Vocabulary 重點單字

- **recover** *v.* 使恢復原狀

  例：This company lost a lot of money during the financial crisis but it has recovered recently.
  這間公司於金融風暴時虧損，但最近已漸漸恢復了。

- **fiddle** *n.* 小提琴（口語）

  例：Victoria's hobby is to play the fiddle.
  Victoria 的嗜好為拉小提琴。

- **illness** *n.* 生病；身體不適

  例：After a long illness, he realized that a health body is the most important thing in his life.
  經過長時間的病痛，他領悟到一個健康的身體為生命中最重要的事。

- **recession** *n.* 經濟蕭條期

  例：After a long period of economic recession, this country is starting to recover.
  經過長時間的經濟蕭條，這個國家開始復甦。

- **forceful** *adj.* 強而有力的

  例：Most politicians are very forceful during debates.
  大多數的政治家在辯論中，皆表現強而有力的。

- **performance** *n.* 表現

  例：This stage show is a brilliant performance.
  這齣舞台劇的表演絕佳。

- **debate** *n.* 辯論

  例：There were several debates about government's education policy.
  有許多關於政府教育政策的辯論會。

文化巧巧說：諺語與外交相關的文化趣事

You can find many interesting phrases to describe healthy in English and Chinese. Alive and kicking, live and kicking, fit as a fiddle, in the pink and 生龍活虎 are good examples. For alive and well and live and kicking, you can easily understand what they mean from their literal meanings. Fit as a fiddle is using a violin as an example. 生龍活虎 is using a dragon and a tiger in the figurative sense.

Go downhill is a phrase with an opposite meaning. It can be used in business status or health. For instance, ***my grandmother is ninety now, her health is starting to go downhill. During the recession, my aunt's business went downhill.***

Apart from healthy, in the pink and vigorous have different meanings. In the pink can be used to express that a business is doing well. Vigorous also means forceful. It can be used to describe a performance, growth or debate. Most English words or phrases have many different definitions. If you understand these meanings, it can help you to use these phrases in a variety of situations.

中英文中皆有許多有趣的成語來形容健康。Alive and kicking、live and kicking、fit as a fiddle、in the pink、和生龍活虎皆是不錯的例子。你可以從 Alive and well 及 live and kicking 的字面上清楚地了解其定義。而 Fit as a fiddle 以小提琴作為例子，生龍活虎則是以龍和虎來比喻。

Go downhill 為反義字。它可用於生意、或是健康狀況。舉例來說，我的祖母已經九十歲了。她的健康已經開始走下坡了。在經濟蕭條期，我阿姨的公司營運開始走下坡。

除了健康外，In the pink 和 vigorous 也有不同的定義。In the pink 可以用來表達公司經營不錯。Vigorous 則可表示強而有力的。像是形容表現、成長、或辯論等。大部分的英文詞句有多重的定義。假如你能全面了解這些詞句的定義，它可以幫助你運用於各式各樣的情況。

Cut to the chase
開門見山

How to use this idiom and on what occasions you can use this idiom
這句諺語你會怎麼說、能派上用場的場合

Track 53

This phrase was derived from the US film industry in the twentieth century. Cut to the chase originally indicates to get to the interesting chase scene in the film. It means that don't waste time on the unimportant things and focus on the important things. This phrase has been widely used since it was created. This is similar to Chinese phrases - 開門見山 and 切入正題.

這句慣用語於二十世紀時起源於美國的電影產業。**Cut to the chase** 原本指剪輯電影到精采的追逐鏡頭。它比喻著不要浪費時間在不重要的事物上，直接專注於重要的事情。自從發明以來，就廣泛地被使用。這也與中文的開門見山及切入正題相似。

Synonyms and Analysis 中西諺語應用與翻譯

The original idiom 原來怎麼說

Cut to the chase

Synonyms 還能怎麼翻

Get to the point, focus on the important thing, go directly to the important parts, deal with the important matter

Explanations 中西諺語翻譯說明

Another way to describe cut to the chase is getting to the point. When you say get to the point in a conversation, it means to talk about the important matter or the purpose of conversation. People usually say "getting to the point" when time nearly runs out. You can also describe this phrase in a simple way, such as "focus on the important thing", "go directly to the important parts" or "deal with the important matter".

For example, you are taking too much time and focus on the irrelevant issues. Let's deal with the important matter. I'm going to skip unimportant pages and go directly to the important part.

另一個 Cut to the chase 的形容法為 Get to the point。當你於會話中提到 Get to the point，表示請說重要的部分，或本次會話的目的。人們通常於時間快耗盡時，提到 Get to the point。也可以用簡單的方法來形容，像是 Focus on the important thing、go directly to the important parts 或者是 deal with the important matter。

舉例來說，你花太多時間在不相關的議題上。讓我們來處理重要的事吧！我要跳過不重要的頁面，直接提到重要的部分。

Notes

Analysis 中西諺語翻譯分析

Cut to the chase and get to the point are used as single phrases in sentences. Examples can go like this: ***Let's stop talking about the irrelevant subjects and cut to the chase. I am about to go to a meeting, please get to the point.***

Focus on the important thing, go directly to the important parts and deal with the important matter can be put after subjects in sentences. Examples can go like this: ***I am afraid we don't have time to go through all the details. Let's focus on the important thing.***

Cut to the chase 及 get to the point 在句子中作為單一片語使用。舉例來說，***我們別再說不相關的話題了，切入主題吧。我準備要去開會了，請直接講重點。***

Focus on the important thing、go directly to the important parts 及 deal with the important matter 在句子中置於主詞後面。例子如下：***我很遺憾，我們沒有時間討論所有的細節。請專注在重點吧。***

FAQ 中西文化外交交流的一問三答 Track 54

Q How do you describe "cut to the chase" in Chinese?

請問如何用中文形容 *cut to the chase* 呢？

❶ There are many ways to describe "cut to the chase" in Chinese. 開門見山 is a good example. 開門見山 is described in a figurative sense. Its literal meaning is opening the door and seeing the mountain. It denotes "getting to the point".

中文中有許多方法可形容 cut to the chase，像是開門見山就是一個很好的例子。開門見山是以比喻的方式來形容。它字面上的意思為打開門就看見山。這也暗示直接切入重點。

❷ Um, you can say 言歸正傳. It means stop talking about irrelevant subjects and go back to the main issue.

嗯，你可以說言歸正傳。它的意思為停止再說不相關的話題，直接回到主題吧。

❸ Well, you can simply say 切入正題. It indicates going directly to the main topic.

簡單來說，就是切入正題。它表示直接進入主要的議題。

Q What kind of situations can you use these Chinese phrases?

在什麼情況下，可使用這些中文的成語？

❶ For 開門見山, it is usually used in a situation where you want someone to go directly to the main issue in the conversation.

就開門見山而言，它通常用於某人想要將話題直接導入主題。

❷ If you have been talking about irrelevant topics for a long time and want to go to the important subject, you can say 言歸正傳.

假如你已經在談了很久不相關的話題，並想要討論重點時，你可以說言歸正傳。

❸ Well, people often use 切入正題 if they feel someone doesn't want to get to the point and want to focus on an important topic.

當人們覺得某人說話不直截了當，並想直接專注於重點時，可使用「切入正題」。

Q Can you tell me more about the origin of "cut to the chase"?

請問你可以告訴我更多關於 *cut to the chase* 的起源嗎？

❶ Well, it is originally from the US film industry in the twentieth century. Since it is very useful for the busy lifestyle today, it has been widely used since it was created.

它於二十世紀時，出現於美國的電影業。由於這句慣用語十分的實用，且符合現代人的忙碌生活，它自發明後，就被廣為使用。

❷ It means editing the film in order to watch the exciting part of the film.

它指剪接電影，以直接看電影中最精采的部分。

❸ It has been mentioned many times in the newspaper in the twentieth century and developed to the current meaning of "get to the point".

它於二十世紀時被許多的報紙所提及，也漸漸地演變為現在get to the point的定義。

Vocabulary 重點單字

- **scene** *n.* 電影的鏡頭；場景

例：Her first role in the film was a waitress in a wedding scene.
她在電影中的第一個角色為一名在婚禮場景的服務生。

- **focus on** *v.* 集中於

例：I'm going to focus my attention on my study.
我要把我的注意力皆集中於課業上。

- **run out** *v.* 用完

例：John has run out of his money and has to get a job.
John 已花光他的錢，需要找一份工作做。

- **irrelevant** *adj.* 不相關的

例：This report is irrelevant to the purpose of research.
這份報告與本研究的目的不相符。

- **misleading** *adj.* 誤導的

例：This is misleading information. Can you please make corrections?
這是誤導的資訊。可否請你更正？

- **edit** *v.* 剪輯

例：The film has been edited to a short documentary.
這部電影已被剪輯成一部短篇紀錄片。

- **silent film** *n.* 無聲電影

例：Actors and actresses in silent films had excellent performing skills.
無聲電影的男女演員有著絕佳的演技。

- **bush** *n.* 灌木叢

例：Rabbits hide behind bushes in order to escape from foxes.
兔子躲在灌木叢後，以躲避狐狸的追捕。

文化巧巧說：諺語與外交相關的文化趣事

Cut to the chase was originally from the US silent films. As this interesting phrase is very useful for the busy lifestyle nowadays, it has been widely used in a variety of situations. There are many ways to describe cut to the chase in Chinese, such as 開門見山, 言歸正傳 or 切入正題. 開門見山 also describes someone who always gets to the point and let people know what they think.

Chinese phrase - 拐彎抹角 and 兜圈子 are opposite to 開門見山. 拐彎抹角 denotes someone who speaks misleadingly and doesn't want to get to the point. It is similar to an English idiom - beat around the bush. People usually say "Don't beat around the bush" to encourage people to say what they think in their mind.

It is interesting that both Chinese and English have so many phrases in common. When you learn a new phrase, you can also learn its antonym at the same time in order to make a comprehensive conversation.

Cut to the chase 起源於美國電影業。因為它十分合乎現代人的繁忙生活，已被廣泛地使用在各式各樣的情形。中文中有許多 cut to the chase 的形容方法，像是開門見山、言歸正傳，或切入正題。開門見山也形容某人說話方式直接，且總是讓別人知道他在想什麼。

中文慣用語－拐彎抹角、及兜圈子與開門見山相反。拐彎抹角表示著某人說話方式模糊不直接。它也與英文成語 beat around the bush 類似。一般人通常用 don't beat around the bush 來鼓勵他人說出心中所想講的話。

有趣的是，中英文的慣用語中有這麼多的相似之處。當你學習一個新的慣用語時，也可以同時了解其反義字，以利增加話題的豐富性。

Unit 8

Down in the dumps
鬱鬱寡歡

How to use this idiom and on what occasions you can use this idiom
這句諺語你會怎麼說、能派上用場的場合

Track 55

Down in the dumps is a colloquial expression describing someone who is unhappy or depressed. The word "dumps" appeared in the early sixteenth century and has been widely used in plays. It appeared in Shakespeare's plays many times. Down in the dumps is similar to a Chinese phrase -鬱鬱寡歡.

Down in the dumps 為描述某人不快樂或沮喪的口語表達方式。Dumps 最早出現於十六世紀初，並廣泛地使用於戲劇中。它曾多次出現於莎士比亞的戲劇中。Down in the dumps 也與中文的鬱鬱寡歡不謀而同。

Synonyms and Analysis 中西諺語應用與翻譯

01 chapter
02 chapter
03 chapter
04 chapter

The original idiom 原來怎麼說

Down in the dumps

Synonyms 還能怎麼翻

Down in the mouth, unhappy, depressed, melancholy, dejected, sad, moody

Explanations 中西諺語翻譯說明

There are many simple ways to describe down in the dumps in English, such as sad, unhappy, depressed, melancholy or dejected. Examples can go like this: ***It's so sad to see so many homeless people on the street. Kate looked dejected when she learned some bad news this afternoon.*** Apart from being sad, moody also indicates someone who becomes unhappy easily. For example, ***Emily is so moody. She was happy five minutes ago but has become angry all of a sudden.*** Moody is similar to 喜 怒 無 常 in Chinese.

英語中有許多形容 down in the dumps 的表達方式，像是 sad、unhappy、depressed、melancholy，或是 dejected。舉例來說，***看到這麼多無家可歸的人真令人難過。Kate 在下午得知壞消息後，就十分地沮喪***。除了表示難過之外，moody 也可以形容某人很容易不開心。舉例來說，***Emily 是如此喜怒無常。她五分鐘前還很開心，但突然地生氣了***。Moody 也與中文的喜怒無常相似。

unhappy *adj.* 不高興的	**depressed** *adj.* 沮喪的
homeless *adj.* 無家可歸的	**match** *n.* 比賽
financial situation 財務狀況	

Analysis 中西諺語翻譯分析

Down in the dumps is used as a single phrase in sentences and usually comes with a bit. An example can go like this: ***Johnny was a bit down in the dumps after his favorite football team lost the match last night.*** Unhappy, depressed, melancholy, dejected, sad and moody are used as adjectives in sentences. Examples can go like this: ***Judy seemed depressed about her financial situation. After her husband passed away, she became a melancholy woman.***

Down in the dumps 在句子中作為單一片語，且通常跟隨著 a bit。它的例子為：***Johnny 昨晚在他最喜愛的足球隊輸球後，感到有點沮喪***。Unhappy、depressed、melancholy、dejected、sad 及 moody 在句子中作為形容詞。舉例來說：***Judy 似乎對她的財務狀況有些沮喪。自從她的丈夫過去後，她成為一位鬱鬱寡歡的女人。***

FAQ 中西文化外交交流的一問三答 Track 56

Q ***What are antonyms of down in the dumps?***
Down in the dumps 的反義字為何？

❶ There are many ways to describe antonyms of down in the dumps, such as over the moon. It indicates someone is extremely happy. This is a colloquial expression.

有許多的方式來形容 Down in the dumps 的反義字，像是 over the moon。它指某人極開心。這是一個口語化的表達方法。

❷ Well, you can say "jump for joy". It means very happy when someone hears a piece of good news.

你可以說 jump for joy。它形容當某人聽到一個好消息時，十分高興的樣子。

❸ In seventh heaven is a good expression describing someone who is delighted.

In seventh heaven 為一個很好的表達方式。它描述某人非常快樂的樣子。

Q Could you give me more examples about the antonyms of down in the dumps?

請問可以給我更多關於 *Down in the dumps* 反義字的例子嗎？

❶ Here is an example for over the moon. The whole country was over the moon when their national team won the football game.

這裡有個 Over the moon 的例子。當國家隊贏得這場足球賽時，整個國家欣喜若狂。

❷ Um, let me think. You can say Gary jumped for joy when he heard he passed an important exam.

讓我想想看。你可以說當 Gary 聽到他通過了一個重要的考試時，他非常高興。

❸ Well, I'd be in seventh heaven if I had won the lottery.

假如我贏得樂透，我會開心極了。

Q *Why did they use dumps in this phrase?*
為什麼在這句慣用語中使用 *Dumps*？

❶ Well, this was common to describe dumps as depression in medieval times.

在中古世紀時，使用 Dumps 來形容沮喪是很常見的。

❷ Down in the dumps appeared in a dictionary in the late eighteenth century.

Down in the dumps 於十八世紀末出現於一個字典裡。

❸ It means dejected. It has been used in Shakespeare's plays many times since the sixteenth century.

它表示沮喪的。它從十六世紀以來，曾多次引用於莎士比亞的戲劇中。

Vocabulary 重點單字

- **melancholy** *adj.* 憂鬱的

  例：Cold weather gives him a feeling of melancholy.
  冷天氣使他覺得憂鬱。

- **moody** *adj.* 悶悶不樂的

  例：She has been moody all afternoon since she lost her wallet.
  自從她遺失了皮包後，她一整個下午悶悶不樂的。

- **all of a sudden** *adv.* 突然地

  例：All of a sudden, a cat turned up in the middle of the road and caused a car accident.
  一隻貓突然地出現在路中央，並造成車禍。

- **pass away** *v.* 去世

  例：His grandfather passed away last night.
  他的爺爺於昨晚過世。

- **medieval** *adj.* 中世紀的

  例：This is a famous medieval town in Europe.
  這是一個知名的歐洲中世紀城鎮。

- **well-known** *adj.* 眾所周知的

  例：She is a well-known businesswoman in Asia.
  她是亞洲眾所周知的女商人。

- **happy camper** *n.* 滿意現況的人

  例：Maggie has failed three exams. She is not a happy camper.
  Maggie 三科考試不及格。她現在可是不滿意現況。

- **dejected** *adj.* 沮喪的

  例：Steven was dejected because his first interview didn't go well.
  因為 Steven 的第一場面試不順利，他感到沮喪。

文化巧巧說：諺語與外交相關的文化趣事

Down in the dumps is a well-known expression describing depression. It has been commonly used since the sixteenth century. There are many similar phrases in Chinese, such as 愁眉苦臉, 愁眉不展, 鬱鬱寡歡 or 悶悶不樂.

Both 鬱鬱寡歡 and 悶悶不樂 indicate someone is depressed. 愁眉苦臉 and 愁眉不展 are used in a figurative sense. It denotes that someone looks miserable. They are commonly used in daily conversation. 洋洋得意 is opposite to down in the dumps in Chinese.

There are many antonyms of down in the dumps in English, such as over the moon or happy camper. A happy camper means a happy person but it is usually used in the negative way. For example, ***Lucy has just lost her wallet and phone. She is not a happy camper now.***

Down in the dumps 為形容沮喪的一個知名慣用語。它於十六世紀以來就被廣泛地使用。中文中也有許多類似的慣用語，像是愁眉苦臉、愁眉不展、鬱鬱寡歡、或悶悶不樂。

鬱鬱寡歡及悶悶不樂皆是指某人很消沉的。愁眉苦臉、愁眉不展則是在比喻的意義上使用。它指某人看起來不快樂的。這些慣用語也常用於生活會話中。中文的洋洋得意則與 Down in the dumps 相反。

英語中有許多的方式來表達 Down in the dumps 的反義字，像是 over the moon 或 happy camper。Happy camper 指一個快樂的人，但此慣用語通常以負面的方式表達。比如說，Lucy 剛剛遺失了皮包和手機，她現在可是不滿意現況。

In the doghouse
麻煩大了

How to use this idiom and on what occasions you can use this idiom
這句諺語你會怎麼說、能派上用場的場合

Track 57

In the doghouse means that someone is in great trouble. In the doghouse first appeared in print in the early twentieth century. This phrase began to be used widely in the United States since the early twentieth century. People usually use this phrase when they try to express someone is unhappy with them because they have done something wrong. This is a colloquial expression and is similar to 麻煩大了 or 惹麻煩 in Chinese.

In the doghouse 指某人惹了大麻煩了。In the doghouse 於二十世紀初時首次出現，並於美國開始被廣泛地使用。人們通常用這句慣用語來表示自己因犯錯，而使他人對其不滿。這是一句口語化的表達方式，並且與中文的麻煩大了，或惹麻煩相似。

Synonyms and Analysis 中西諺語應用與翻譯

The original idiom 原來怎麼說

In the doghouse

Synonyms 還能怎麼翻

In someone's bad books, in someone's bad graces, out of favor with someone, in disgrace, in trouble

Explanations 中西諺語翻譯說明

Another way to describe this phrase is in someone's bad books. If you are in someone's bad books, it means that you have done something bad and made someone feel unhappy. For example, ***he is in Hannah's bad books because he broke her favorite vase.*** It can be called as in someone's bad graces. There are many simple ways to describe in the doghouse in English, such as out of favor with someone, in disgrace or in trouble.

另一個描述此句的慣用語為 In someone's bad books。假如你在某人的 Bad books 裡，它表示你做了一些壞事，並使某人不悅。舉例來說，***Hannah 對他很惱火，因為他打破 Hannah 最喜愛的花瓶***。它也可以稱為 in someone's bad graces。英語中有許多方法來形容 in the doghouse， 像是 out of favor with someone、in disgrace 或者是 in trouble。

doghouse *n.* 狗屋	**In someone's bad books** 不討某人的喜歡
Out of favor with someone 不受某人的喜愛	**break** *v.* 打破
in trouble 麻煩大了	**crash** *v.* 撞壞
fail *v.* 不及格	

Analysis 中西諺語翻譯分析

In the doghouse is used as a single phrase in sentences. An example can go like this: ***Robert is in the doghouse because he crashed his wife's new car.*** In someone's bad books is usually put after verbs in sentences. For instance, ***Helen is in a teacher's bad books because she failed the exams again.***

In disgrace and in trouble are usually put after verbs in sentences. Examples can go like this: ***Nicole is in disgrace with her mother because she dropped out of university. If we don't go home before midnight, we'll be in trouble.***

In the doghouse 在句中作為單一片語使用。比如說，***Robert 惹了大麻煩了，因為他撞壞了他太太的新車。*** In someone's bad books 通常於句中置於動詞後。比如說，***Helen 不被老師所滿意，因為她考試又不及格。***

In disgrace 及 in trouble 一般在句子中置於動詞之後。舉例來說，***Nicole 因從大學退學，而使她的母親蒙羞。若我們不在午夜前回家，我們就麻煩大了。***

FAQ 中西文化外交交流的一問三答 Track 58

Q ***How do you describe in the doghouse in Chinese?***
請問如何用中文來描述 *In the doghouse*？

❶ Well, in the doghouse means 因犯錯而受到冷落 in Chinese.

In the doghouse 在中文中指因犯錯而受到冷落。

❷ "In the doghouse" is colloquial. If you want to describe it in a colloquial way, you can say 麻煩大了or 惹麻煩 in Chinese.

In the doghouse 為口語用法。假如你想用中文口語的方式來表達，你可以說麻煩大了，或惹麻煩。

❸ Um, 失寵 is another way to describe out of favor with someone in Chinese.

失寵為 Out of favor with someone 的中文用法。

Q What are antonyms of in the doghouse?
In the doghouse的反義字為何？

❶ Well, you can say in someone's good books. If you have done something good and make someone like you, you are in someone's good book.

你可以用 In someone's good books 來表達。假如你做了一些好事，並讓他人喜歡你時，你就是 in someone's good book。

❷ You can also say in someone's good graces. It is the same as in someone's good books.

你可以說 In someone's good graces。它與 In someone's good books相同。

❸ "In someone's favor" is a good example. If you are in someone's favor, you are liked by someone.

In someone's favor 是一個很好的例子。假如你是 in someone's favor，你便被他人所喜愛。

Q Could you please give me more examples about these phrases?

請問你可以舉更多關於這些慣用語的例子嗎？

❶ Here is an example for in someone's good books. Paul is in his grandmother's good books because he helped her to move house.

這裡有個 In someone's good books 的例子。Paul 的奶奶對他很滿意，因為他幫忙搬家。

❷ Everyone in the company tries to get in the boss's good graces in order to get promoted.

公司裡的每個人都試著討老闆的歡心，以獲得升遷的機會。

❸ This candidate is likely to win this election because he is currently in people's favor.

這位候選人可能會贏得這場選舉，因為他目前受人民喜愛。

Vocabulary 重點單字

- **disgrace** *n.* 丟臉

  例：She brought disgrace on the family by telling a lie.
  她說謊的行為讓家人丟臉。

- **vase** *n.* 花瓶

  例：You need to put more water in the vase.
  你需要在花瓶裡盛更多水。

- **candidate** *n.* 候選人

  例：There are three candidates for the presidential election.
  有三名候選人參加總統大選。

- **election** *n.* 選舉

  例：There are less voters in this year's election.
  今年選舉的投票者少很多。

- **annoy** *v.* 使生氣

  例：I was annoyed with my brother for his rude behavior.
  我弟弟無禮的行為使我生氣。

- **drop out** *v.* 退學

  例：Mary dropped out of school and ran a restaurant.
  Mary從學校退學並經營一間餐廳。

- **midnight** *n.* 午夜

  例：He worked until midnight and left the office.
  他加班到午夜才離開辦公室。

- **make the most of something** *v.* 盡量利用

  例：She will study in Europe for one year. She wants to make the most of her time when she studies in Europe.
  她將會在歐洲學習一年。她想要她在歐洲學習時充份利用時間。

文化巧巧說：諺語與外交相關的文化趣事

In the doghouse is used in a figurative sense. It indicates that you annoy someone because of something you have done or said. It is a colloquial expression and has been widely used since it was created.

In someone's bad books is another similar expression. It uses books in a figurative sense. The use of bad books indicates disfavor. The other relevant phrases are in someone's good books, in someone's good/ bad graces and in someone's black books.

There are many ways to describe in the doghouse in Chinese, such as 受冷落 or 失寵. It means out of favor with someone. People usually use 受冷落 or 失寵 to describe they are no longer preferred by someone.

Understanding the relevant phrases prevents you from repeating yourself. It helps you to make the most of your conversation with your clients or friends.

In the doghouse 為在比喻的意義上使用。它指因你做了某些事、或說了某些話而使某人生氣。這是個口話化的表達方式，並且自發明以來，就被廣泛地使用。

In someone's bad books 為另一種類似的用法。它使用書本做為比喻。Bad books 意指不受人喜歡。其他相關的慣用語為 In someone's good books、in someone's good/ bad graces 及 in someone's black books。

中文有許多形容法來描述 in the doghouse，像是受冷落、或失寵。它指不受某人喜歡。人們通常用受冷落、或失寵來表示他們不再被某人所重視。

了解更多相關語可以避免一直重覆使用相同的詞句，並可幫助你有效地運用於與客戶或朋友的對話中。

Unit 10 Up the creek without a paddle 處於困境

How to use this idiom and on what occasions you can use this idiom 這句諺語你會怎麼說、能派上用場的場合

Track 59

Up the creek without a paddle is described in a figurative sense. The literal meaning of "up the creek without a paddle" is someone being in a boat in a small river without a paddle. It denotes that someone is in a hopeless situation. For instance, ***the financial crisis has made many people feel like they are up the creek without a paddle.*** This phrase is similar to a Chinese phrase called 處於困境.

Up the creek without a paddle 是用比喻的意義使用。它字面上的意思為處於河流中的一條沒有槳的小船上。它象徵著某人處於一個絕望的情形。舉例來說，金融風暴讓許多人處於絕望的狀況。這個慣用語也與中文的處於困境類似。

Synonyms and Analysis 中西諺語應用與翻譯

01 chapter
02 chapter
03 chapter
04 chapter

The original idiom 原來怎麼說

Up the creek without a paddle

Synonyms 還能怎麼翻

Up the creek, up shit creek without a paddle, out on a limb, helpless, powerless

Explanations 中西諺語翻譯說明

Up the creek without a paddle can be called as up the creek or up shit creek without a paddle. Up shit creek without a paddle is a slang phrase. Out on a limb is also similar to up the creek without a paddle. It denotes that someone is in an isolated and dangerous position and lacks support. Alternatively, you can simply say helpless or powerless to describe this phrase.

Up the creek without a paddle 又稱為 up the creek，或者是 up shit creek without a paddle。Up shit creek without a paddle 則為俚語。Out on a limb 也與 Up the creek without a paddle 相似。它表示某人處於一個孤立、充滿危機、而且缺乏幫助的情況。或者，也可用簡單的表達方法，像是 helpless 或 powerless。

paddle *n.* 槳	**out on a limb** 孤立的
helpless *adj.* 無助的	**powerless** *adj.* 無能力的
slang *n.* 俚語	**lack** *v./n.* 缺少
unpopular *adj.* 不受歡迎的	**witness** *v.* 目擊

Analysis 中西諺語翻譯分析

Up the creek is often used as a single phrase and put after verbs in sentences. For example, ***his car broke down in the middle of nowhere. He is up the creek without a paddle.***

Out on a limb usually comes with go in sentences. An example can go like this: ***She went out on a limb and chose an unpopular party.***

Helpless and powerless are often used as adjectives in sentences. For instance, ***I feel helpless because there is nothing I can do to change this situation. Peter witnessed the car accident but he was powerless to do anything at that time.***

Up the creek 在句中通常作為單一片語，並置於動詞之後。比方說，***他的車子在偏僻的地方發生故障了，他陷入為難的困境中。***

Out on a limb 通常在句子中與 Go 共用。它的例子為：***她選擇處境危險且不受歡迎的政黨。***

Helpless 和 Powerless 通常於句子中當作形容詞使用。例如，***我感到絶望，因為無論我做什麼事也無法改變這個狀況。Peter 目擊這場車禍，但當時他無力去做任何事。***

FAQ 中西文化外交交流的一問三答 Track 60

Q *What is the difference between up the creek without a paddle and out on a limb?*

請問 *Up the creek without a paddle* 及 *Out on a limb* 有何差別？

❶ Well, both up the creek without a paddle and out on a limb mean being in an awkward situation. However, out on a limb is often used to express someone who lacks support.

Up the creek without a paddle 及 Out on a limb 都是在形容處於難以應付的情況。但是 Out on a limb 通常用來表達某人缺乏支援。

❷ Um, let me think. Up the creek without a paddle usually describes someone is in a predicament.

嗯，讓我想想看。Up the creek without a paddle 通常形容某人處於窘境之中。

❸ If you go out on a limb, you support something which is unpopular.

假如你 Go out on a limb，你支持一些不受歡迎的事物。

Q What do you describe up the creek without a paddle in Chinese?

如何用中文形容*Up the creek without a paddle*？

❶ You can use 處於困境 to describe up the creek without a paddle. 處於困境 means being in a difficult situation.

你可以用處於困境來形容 Up the creek without a paddle。處於困境指處在一個左右為難的情況。

❷ 陷入窘境 is a good example. It indicates being in a predicament.

陷入窘境是一個好的例子。它表示處於一個難以應付的困境中。

❸ Alternatively, you can say 孤立無援. It means being in an isolated and helpless position.

或者，也可以說孤立無援。它意指處在一個孤立且無助的情形。

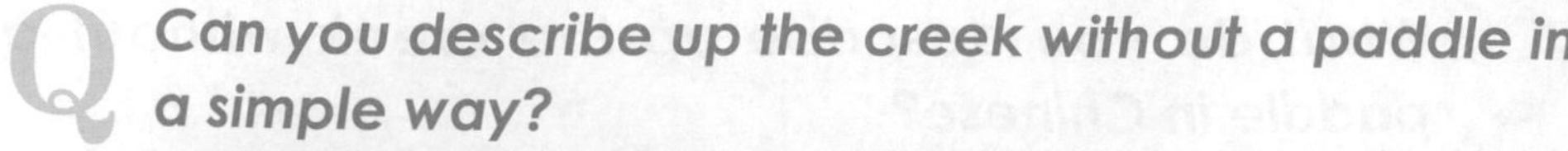

Q *Can you describe up the creek without a paddle in a simple way?*

請問你可以用簡單的方式來形容 *Up the creek without a paddle*嗎？

❶ Yes, you can. You can simply say being left without any help.

是的，可以。你可說被留在一個沒有任何支援的環境。

❷ Um, let me think. There is an easy way to describe up the creek without a paddle. Someone is in a situation of helplessness.

嗯，讓我想想。有一個簡單描述 Up the creek without a paddle 的方法，即某人處於一個無助的情況。

❸ Well, someone is in a difficult situation and has no support from other people.

某人在難以應付的情況中，並且沒有任何人的幫助。

Vocabulary 重點單字

- **creek** *n.* 小河；小溪

  例：There is a Café near the creek. Do you want to go there and have a rest?
  在小河旁邊有一間咖啡館，要不要去哪裡休息一下。

- **limb** *n.* 樹枝

  例：Don't climb a tree and strain a limb. It's dangerous.
  別爬樹及拉樹枝。這很危險。

- **isolated** *adj.* 被孤立的

  例：He has no friends and this makes him feel isolated.
  他沒有朋友，這讓他覺得自己被孤立了。

- **alternatively** *adv.* 或者

  例：We can go shopping, or alternatively, we can stay at home watching TV.
  我們可以去購物，或者我們可以留在家裡看電視。

- **break down** *v.* 故障

  例：His car broke down on the motorway.
  他的車在高速公路上故障了。

- **in the middle of nowhere** *ph.* 在偏僻的地方

  例：My father has a summer house in the middle of nowhere.
  我的父親在一處偏僻的地方，擁有一個暑假渡假小屋。

- **awkward** *adj.* 難處理的

  例：This is an awkward situation and not everyone can handle it.
  這個難處理的情況，並不是每個人都能應付。

文化巧巧說：諺語與外交相關的文化趣事

Both up the creek without a paddle and out on a limb are used in a figurative sense and describe similar situations. Up the creek without a paddle denotes being in a boat without a paddle. The literal meaning of out on a limb is to climb a tree. It describes a situation where someone should go and reach the apple or worry about the branch might break. It denotes that someone is in a disadvantage position and has no support.

This is close to a Chinese idiom called 孤立無援. It means do something alone without any help. 孤立無援 is also similar to many English phrases, such as leave someone high and dry or throw someone back on their own resources. Leave someone high and dry originally means boats were beached. It indicates that being left in a helpless situation. Throw someone back on their own resources indicates someone has been forced to be independent without any help from other people.

These phrases have something in common but are derived from different backgrounds. This is an interesting point and you can share it with your clients and friends.

Up the creek without a paddle 和 out on a limb 皆是使用比喻的方式形容類似的處境。Up the creek without a paddle 表示停留在一條無槳的船上。而 Out on a limb 字面上意思為爬樹。它形容某人爬樹時，是否要摘水果或者擔心樹枝會折斷。這是暗示著某人處在孤立且不利的處境。

Out on a limb 也與中文的孤立無援不謀而同。它表示獨立處理某事，且無外來的援助。孤立無援也與許多的英文慣用語相似，像是 Leave someone high and dry 、或是 throw someone back on their own resources。Leave someone high and dry 原本是指船隻被拖上岸。它暗示著處於一個無助的情況。Throw someone back on their own resources 表示某人被迫學習獨立，且無他人的援助。

這些慣用語有許多共通之處，但是源自不同的背景。這也是你可以和客户及朋友分享的有趣話題。

Leader 037

Smart 外交英語：從中西諺語的文化交流開始

作　　者　詹宜婷
發 行 人　周瑞德
執行總監　齊心瑀
企劃編輯　饒美君
校　　對　編輯部
封面構成　高鍾琪

內頁構成　好映像有限公司
印　　製　大亞彩色印刷製版股份有限公司
初　　版　2016 年 03 月
定　　價　新台幣 380 元
出　　版　力得文化
電　　話　(02) 2351-2007
傳　　真　(02) 2351-0887
地　　址　100 台北市中正區福州街 1 號 10 樓之 2
E-mail　best.books.service@gmail.com
網　　址　www.bestbookstw.com

港澳地區總經銷　泛華發行代理有限公司
地　　址　香港新界將軍澳工業邨駿昌街 7 號 2 樓
電　　話　(852) 2798-2323
傳　　真　(852) 2796-5471

國家圖書館出版品預行編目資料

Smart 外交英語：從中西諺語的文化交流開始 /
詹宜婷著. -- 初版. -- 臺北市 : 力得文化,
2016.03
面 ; 公分. -- (Leader ; 37)
ISBN 978-986-92398-5-1(平裝附光碟片)

1.英語 2.諺語

805.128　　104027861

Lead your way. Be your own leader!

Lead your way. Be your own leader!